Death by Proxy

A DIY Diva Mystery

by

Paula Darnell

For information, email Cozy Cat Press, cozycatpress@aol.com or visit our website at: www.cozycatpress.com

COZY CAT
PRESS

ISBN: 978-1-946063-89-2
Printed in the United States of America

10 9 8 7 6 5 4 3 2 1

To my wonderful daughter Sara with much love and many thanks for her steadfast encouragement of my mystery writing

Chapter 1

"Duane Harris Wesson! Is *that* your idea of a proposal?"

If I'd been standing, I'd have put my hands on my hips, but I was sitting beside Wes on the sofa in my den.

He'd just suggested that a riverboat cruise on the Mississippi would make a great honeymoon, but he hadn't asked me to marry him!

"Uh, definitely not." My boyfriend grabbed a pillow, placed it on the tile floor in front of me, and knelt on the plush cushion. He took my hand. "Laurel, sweetheart, I love you, and I'd love for us to spend the rest of our lives together."

He fumbled in his jacket pocket for a moment before pulling out a small velvet-covered box. He opened it and took out a spectacular diamond ring. "Will you marry me?"

"Yes!" I said breathlessly, and Wes slipped the stunning ring onto my finger.

Bear, my chocolate Labrador retriever, had been snoozing on his bed in front of the fireplace, but sensing that something was up and not wanting to be left out, he came over and sat in front of me, next to Wes, and put his head on my lap.

Wes put one arm around me and the other around Bear, as I leaned forward to kiss him.

"Think I can get up now?" Wes asked.

"Yes."

"Good," He rose and sat beside me. "That's a relief.

When you called me by all three of my names, I knew I had to up my game. When I was a kid, my mom used to say that to me when I was in trouble."

"Well, you're redeemed. Not many men would tolerate a dog nudging his way into a proposal. You're a very special man, and I love you madly."

Wes took me in his arms, and we managed a proper kiss before Bear began gently prodding us with his nose.

"Don't worry, Bear," Wes reassured him, as he scratched behind the inquisitive dog's ears. "You'll always be part of our family."

*****

In the weeks that followed Wes's proposal, I often found myself holding up my left hand to admire my engagement ring. The rose gold ring, encrusted with small channel-set diamonds swirled gracefully around a large diamond solitaire, and I never tired of looking at it.

As for more practical matters, Wes and I had decided that we'd buy a house. Wes had lived in the same spartan two-bedroom downtown Center City apartment for years, and although I'd bought a house when I moved to Iowa from Seattle three years ago, I didn't have a guest room.

I had converted one spare bedroom into my office and the other into my craft room. Because my DIY Diva business involves developing craft projects for classes I teach at the Hawkeye Haven community center and writing books about them, I really needed those rooms.

Whenever my parents visited from Seattle, they stayed at my cousin Tracey's house, located just a short jaunt away in our walled, guard-gated community,

Hawkeye Haven. Tracey's not only my cousin, but also my BFF as well, so the arrangement had worked out well, but now that Wes and I planned to marry, his son Derek, a medical student at Johns Hopkins, would need a place to stay when he visited.

Wes and I were both excited at the prospect of finding our new home, but it was proving a bit more difficult than we'd anticipated. As a detective in the robbery and homicide division of the Center City Police Department, he worked long hours, and we'd had to cancel a few appointments with Lisa, our real estate agent, because of last-minute work conflicts. Most of the houses we'd looked at didn't suit us for one reason or another, but we were determined to persevere with our search until we could find a home that both of us really liked. We wanted a big backyard, too, so that Bear would have plenty of room to roam and to play the games of fetch that he loved so much.

Much to our real estate agent's chagrin, we'd told her that we were in no hurry. After our wedding, we'd live in my house until we found the perfect new home.

Planning our wedding was turning out to be much easier than finding a new house. We'd both agreed that we'd prefer a simple, informal wedding at home with just family and a few friends in attendance. I'd made my own gown, a bias-cut, 1930s-inspired style in robin's egg blue silk charmeuse, and it hung in my closet, waiting for the Big Day, now only a couple of weeks away.

Tracey had volunteered to make the luncheon food for the reception. Since she's a gourmet cook, I knew it would be fantastic. As for the cake, my friends Amy and Cynthia wanted to make it for us. Just last week, we'd had a sample tasting of the lemon-filled cake that they were planning to bake and pronounced it scrumptious.

My neighbors Liz and Fran would be making me a bridal bouquet from fresh flowers picked the morning of the wedding, and they had volunteered to take care of all the other flower arrangements. Our wedding was scheduled for mid-June, the day before we would depart for our Mississippi riverboat cruise, so it would be too late for the lovely lavender lilacs that so many Hawkeye Haven residents had in their yards. The peonies would be gone by then, too, but Liz and Fran were both keeping a close eye on their gardens and would use whichever beautiful blossoms looked best on the day of the wedding.

As I drove to my class at Hawkeye Haven's community center, I smiled as I thought about how well our wedding plans were coming along. This particular class would be the last in my series of DIY Bridal Crafts classes, as well as the last one I taught before the wedding. My new classes wouldn't begin until a week after Wes and I returned from our honeymoon.

I arrived early and set up the projects that I was going to demonstrate. During previous sessions, we'd made wedding jewelry, favors, invitations, silk flowers, bouquets, corsages, and boutonnières. Today, I planned to show my students how to make a birdcage veil and a crystal-and-pearl hair vine with gold or silver wire. After I put my samples on the long table in front of the classroom, I turned on the computer and the projector so that I could show the students a brief step-by-step tutorial on both projects.

When I'd pitched my idea for a DIY Bridal Crafts class to Colette, Hawkeye Haven's property manager, she'd been enthusiastic. We both knew there might be limited interest, but we were pleasantly surprised when a dozen Hawkeye Haven residents enrolled in the course. The class consisted of a few brides-to-be and several relatives of others.

I'd just finished setting up my demonstration projects when the first two students arrived.

"Hi, Laurel," my friend Amber greeted me. "I can't believe this is our last class. It's gone so fast."

"Yes, it has," I agreed.

"Where does the time go?" Alice, Amber's ninety-year-old neighbor, said wistfully. "Nothing we can do about that, I guess."

"Are you feeling all right, Alice?" I asked because she didn't seem like her usual sprightly self.

"Sorry, girls," she said. "I'm fine. I'll just miss everybody."

"What do you mean?" Amber asked. She looked as surprised as I did. Surely Alice's family hadn't convinced her to move into a nursing home. Alice might be plagued by poor eyesight, but she was as active as ever.

"Oh, I'm going to spend the summer with the kids in Montana. My daughter and son-in-law like to get away from the sticky Iowa summers, so this year they rented a big house for the entire family. It should be lots of fun, but they want to leave this weekend. I'm sorry, Laurel, but I'm going to miss both your shower and your wedding."

I hugged her. "I completely understand. Don't worry, Alice; we'll text you some pictures."

"Really?"

"Of course."

"You won't forget?"

"I'm taking lots of pictures at the wedding myself," Amber said, "and by the time you get back, I'll bet Laurel will have her wedding album done, and you can see that, too."

"Thanks, girls." Alice beamed.

Twenty-five-year-old Amber, who worked at home as a website designer, was like a granddaughter to Alice. Besides accompanying her to crafts classes, Amber often drove Alice around town on her errands. When people saw them together, they usually assumed that Amber was Alice's granddaughter. Although Alice had three granddaughters, none of them lived in Center City.

"I hear some people coming. Dibs on this table!" Alice said, as she plunked her tote bag down on a table in the front of the classroom and pulled out a chair. Amber joined her and began unpacking their supplies.

I greeted the other class members as they arrived. Although there were always many familiar faces in my other DIY classes, Amber and Alice were the only two students I'd known before my DIY Bridal Crafts workshop series began. I was somewhat embarrassed that I had to do a furtive check of my class roster as the women came in to remind myself of their names, but try as I might, I didn't recognize one of the students. The mystery was soon cleared up, though, when Tara, a thirty-year-old with long brown hair, introduced her shy friend Megan and asked me if it would be all right if Megan attended the class with her. Although strictly speaking, community center classes were offered only to Hawkeye Haven residents who officially enrolled for each class, Megan, an unassuming girl with a timid manner, looked as though she might wilt at any moment, and I didn't have the heart to turn her away, so I agreed and began the class.

After I presented the instructions and the students had looked at the finished birdcage veils and hair vines I'd brought, they all began making their own projects as I circulated around the class, checking on their progress and helping them when they encountered problems. Things went smoothly, except for one woman who was making an ivory birdcage veil for her daughter's wedding. Unfortunately, she kept stabbing herself with her sewing needle.

"I just hate hand sewing," she declared, as I applied a bandage to her bleeding finger. "Give me my sewing machine any time."

"Hand sewing's not everyone's cup of tea," I said. Although I enjoyed hand stitching myself, I could understand her feelings. "On the bright side, you're almost done, and your daughter's going to appreciate wearing a veil her mom made especially for her. You could finish it later, if your finger hurts."

"No, I'd just as soon finish today," she said. "Do you really think it looks all right?"

"I think it looks beautiful," I said, and several class members chimed in with encouraging words.

Satisfied, she nodded and returned to her task. In less than five minutes, she'd finished the last few stitches. At about the same time, several other students were completing their veils or hair vines.

I returned to the front of the classroom and pulled out a big suitcase I'd stowed earlier under the front table. Before class started, I'd covered the table where I displayed my demo projects with a dark blue table drape to hide the huge bag.

"Here's a little surprise for everybody," I announced as I held up a small hat box. "It's always nice to have a gift box that can double as a storage box, and I have enough of these for everybody's projects. They'll work for a hair vine as well as for a birdcage veil."

"What cute hat boxes!" the woman who'd repeatedly stabbed her finger exclaimed. The small round boxes were ivory with a white lace overlay. I'd found them in a little out-of-the-way shop the last time Tracey and I had gone shopping in Des Moines.

"I have plenty of tissue paper, too," I said, as I handed boxes to everybody and distributed white tissue paper.

"Great idea," Amber said. She hadn't made anything for herself, but she'd helped Alice make three hair vines, one for each of her granddaughters. Instead of pearls and clear or iridescent crystal beads, Alice had chosen to use only colored, faceted crystal beads in two sizes. She made one vine with black crystals, another with pink, and a third with aqua.

"We have a surprise for you, too, Laurel," Tara said, her blue eyes twinkling. "We all know how much you love to cook."

This statement brought a round of laughter from the entire class. It was a well-known fact that not only did I not enjoy cooking but I was also a terrible at it.

"Seriously, we know you and Wes are both busy people, and we thought you might enjoy some home cooking after you return from your honeymoon," she said, handing me an envelope.

I opened the envelope and found a beautiful best-wishes-on-your-wedding card inside, along with six mini-menu plans. On the back of each little menu card was a date and the notation "prepared by" with the names of two class members.

"We partnered up, so you can have six dinners that you won't have to worry about preparing."

"This is great!" I said. "And I know Wes will love to come home to a home-cooked meal, especially if *I* didn't prepare it!"

Everyone laughed.

"Thank you all so much. It's very thoughtful." I scanned the menus quickly. "I'm getting hungry already, just reading about all this yummy food."

"The dates and menus aren't set in stone, Laurel. Just let us know if you want to change anything."

"I can't imagine that I would," I said. "It all looks perfect!" I was very touched by my students' thoughtfulness, especially considering that I didn't know them very well, except for Amber and Alice, who were the only ones in the class I had invited to the wedding. On the other hand, the students all knew it was going to be a small wedding at home, and the invitations had gone out before this series of DIY Bridal Crafts classes began. "Thank you all, again," I said, with a little catch in my throat. "This has been a wonderful class, and I hope all the brides enjoy the projects you've made."

"Mine aren't for brides," Alice piped up.

"Your granddaughters, too, Alice. I know you made their hair vines for special occasions, and I think they'll be thrilled with them."

"I hope so; otherwise, I put Amber to a lot of unnecessary work." Alice chuckled because Amber had done the lion's share of assembling the hair vines Alice would be giving her granddaughters.

"It was fun," Amber said. "Making these pretty hair vines didn't seem like work at all, but speaking of work, I guess we'd better be heading out. I have a client who wants his new website up and running by tomorrow, so now I'll really have a big job to tackle."

I waved good-bye and thanked the students again for their generosity as they departed. Two women lingered. Heather and Holly were sisters in their fifties, and both their daughters were getting married later in the summer. As I walked over to the table where they sat, I could see that Heather was struggling to attach three white silk flowers she'd make in a previous class to the headband anchoring the birdcage veil she'd made today.

"Need any help?" I asked.

"Oh, Laurel, I think so. These silk flowers keep shifting around, and I'm having trouble getting them in the right place."

"Let's see. Show me how you want them arranged."

Heather pushed the flowers together in a cluster and said, "Like so."

"Okay. Let me grab a piece of white felt."

After I fished around in my project bag, I found what I needed and went back to sit next to Heather.

"We'll temporarily glue the flowers in place, just the way you want them," I said, applying a dab of glue to the base of each flower. "Now let's let that dry for a minute and then sew each flower to the felt. After that, just trim the felt and sew it to the ribbon on the headband."

"Should I put a big knot in the thread now?" she asked, after she'd attached the flowers.

"Well, let's try to hide the knot. Let me see," I said, holding the headband. I ran the needle and thread back and forth through the felt and ribbon several times, then tied a square knot, tucked it under a flower, and trimmed it.

"Thank you!" Heather said. "For some reason, I can never seem to do those delicate little maneuvers with the needle."

"It looks perfect," Holly said.

"So does the hair vine you made," her sister said.

"Thanks." Holly turned to me. "I'm not too crafty, Laurel, but I'm glad you had this class. We're definitely going to be able to use everything we made for the girls' weddings."

"It was fun, too. I admit that I got a little frustrated with this veil, but, now that it's done, I can see that it was worth it."

The sisters reached for their hat boxes.

"I was surprised to see Tara come in with Megan today," commented Heather, as she crumpled some white tissue paper and carefully placed the veil she'd made in the hat box, covering it with more tissue paper.

"Why's that?" Holly asked.

"Well, Megan's mother is Patty, the woman who used to be Hawkeye Haven's property manager, and I don't think I've ever known a more unpleasant woman in my life than Patty." She lowered her voice. "She was fired."

Chapter 2

"I didn't know Patty had any children," I said. Unfortunately, I remembered Patty all too well. She had wanted to fire me and get rid of all the Hawkeye Haven instructors. When she found out that she couldn't void our contracts, she settled for acting nasty and dismissive to us. She was equally unpleasant to the residents, none of whom was sorry to see her go. When Hawkeye Haven's homeowners' association board discovered she'd been involved in a kick-back scheme with the former HOA president, Patty was fired. "Patty looks too young to have a daughter Megan's age. I'm guessing Megan's about twenty."

"Megan just turned twenty-one. I go to water aerobics with Tara, and she told me that she just happened to meet Megan one evening a few weeks ago when they were both swimming laps at the pool," Heather said. "Well, according to Tara, Patty was only sixteen when she had Megan, and she hasn't been much of a mother to her. Megan told Tara that her aunt practically raised her, and she's staying with her now."

"Poor Megan," Holly commented. "I never had any dealings with Patty myself, but I remember some of my neighbors weren't too happy with her."

"Neither were mine. She kept sending out threatening notices to residents who weren't doing anything wrong. She harassed my next-door neighbor Liz and threatened her with fines if she didn't paint her house, but she'd had it painted just a couple years ago, and it looked perfectly fine," I said.

"That sure sounds like Patty," Heather commented.

"I wonder whether Megan's here for a visit," I said.

"I don't know. Tara's kind of taken her under her wing, so to speak. I guess that's why she brought her to class today."

"Well, we'd best be off," Holly urged. "We need to meet the girls at the florist's in a few minutes."

After they left, I packed my table drape and project samples in my large suitcase, turned off the classroom computer, straightened a few chairs, and turned out the lights. I'd been in a good mood until I'd been reminded of my experiences with Patty, but there was no reason to dwell on what had happened in the past.

I tried to forget about it as I drove home, and Bear greeted me with tail-wagging enthusiasm as soon as I came in the door. I quickly changed into my old jeans before a romp and a game of fetch with him in the backyard. By the time we were done, he was panting, and I was perspiring profusely. It was a warm day with high humidity, so as soon as I stepped back into the house, I turned on the air conditioner.

The weather gave me pause about our plan to hold our wedding outside in the backyard. It could turn out to be quite miserable if the temperature and humidity soared. We did have a back-up plan, though. If it rained, we could hold the ceremony in the living room, even though it would be a bit cramped, and we'd have to rearrange the furniture. Obviously, we couldn't control the weather, so we'd have to wait until the Big Day to decide whether or not to hold the wedding outside.

I spent the rest of the afternoon writing project instructions for my next book, *DIY Bridal Crafts,* while Bear snoozed nearby on his bed in my office. The time passed quickly, and I hadn't realized it was getting so late until Bear nudged my arm, then ran to the kitchen, where he proceeded to dance for his supper. After I fed him, and he wandered around the backyard for a while, I showered and changed into an apple green cotton gauze sun dress. I grabbed a lightweight sweater and put it next to my handbag, just in case the air conditioning was cranked up at Tony's, the little restaurant where Wes and I often had dinner when he had to return to work afterwards. Although it was nothing fancy, the food was good, and since it was in a strip mall nearby, it had become our go-to place for a quick dinner.

Wes showed up promptly at six, and Bear greeted him joyously, before I could get near him myself. I pushed the front door shut, as Bear flopped over for his usual tummy rub, and Wes obliged him.

"Every time Bear sees you, he expects a tummy rub," I said. "I'm afraid you've created a monster,"

"Guilty as charged," Wes said, "but what about you? You have to admit he's a little spoiled."

"For sure, but he's still a good boy."

"Yes, he is, aren't you, Bear?"

Bear wagged his tail, as though he agreed completely. He gave us his most winning sad-eyed look as we went out the front door and Wes pulled it closed behind us.

"He certainly has his way of letting us know what's on his mind," Wes mused as we strolled hand-in-hand down my front sidewalk to his car. "Your chariot awaits." He opened the door for me, and I slipped into the passenger seat.

Wes turned on the motor and adjusted the air conditioner, but he didn't pull out from the curb right away.

"All these late nights at work are getting old. I'm

sorry I had to bail on the last appointment we had to look at that house on Clover Lane."

I leaned over to give him a kiss, which he wholeheartedly returned. "Don't worry about that. You didn't miss much. If it had been a property we might consider, I would have let you know right away, but it turned out to be a fixer-upper, and, on top of that, the backyard was about the size of a postage stamp. Even though I told Lisa it wasn't for us, she still tried to sell me on the place."

"I wonder why she insisted on showing it to us?" Wes said, as he pulled out into the street. "We've already told her we weren't in a hurry, that we wanted to find just the right house."

"She's not listening. I'm starting to wonder whether we should work with a different agent."

"That might be a good idea. Do you have anyone else in mind?"

"No, and we're already scheduled to look at a couple of other houses this weekend, remember?"

"Oh, right. Well, let's go ahead and look at them. If one of them turns out to be *the one*, we'll make an offer. If not, maybe we'll find somebody else."

"Sounds like a plan," I agreed. I didn't think I could take too much more of Lisa's aggressive sales tactics. "I'll ask my friends if they know of an agent who's not so high pressure."

"Good idea. Sticking with the first agent we ran into at an open house probably wasn't our best move."

When we arrived at the restaurant, Tony's daughter led us to a booth tucked away in a back corner. We'd come there so often in the past few months that we thought of it as our booth. Wes and I both ordered pasta and a salad, and we munched on crusty garlic bread while we waited for our meals.

"Derek called me today with an update on his summer plans," Wes said. "It's kind of in the good-news-bad-news category."

"What is it, Wes?"

"The good news is that he's been accepted into a special summer internship program. He's going to be working with top-notch specialists who've set up a program to treat serious eye diseases overseas."

"So I'm guessing that means he won't be able to attend the wedding," I said softly.

Wes nodded. "The team is flying out next week. I guess I'm short a best man."

"I'm sorry he can't come, sweetie," I said, as I reached across the table to squeeze his hand, "but it does sound like a wonderful opportunity for him."

"That's true. I'm just disappointed. I was looking forward to seeing him before the wedding."

"I know you were. Maybe we can fly to Baltimore for a visit sometime this fall."

"Oh, I don't know. He's always so busy with classes."

"Then how about after he returns, right before school starts for the fall term?"

Wes nodded. "Maybe that would work, and I can ask Dad to be my best man."

Only a few months earlier, Wes's father had suffered a serious heart attack, but his doctor had pronounced him recovered now. He'd returned to his usual routine, except for a mandated change in his diet that he wasn't exactly thrilled about, according to Wes's mother.

"I'm sure he'd be happy to stand up for you."

Wes nodded. "I'll call him later. When I told him about our engagement, it was actually his idea that I ask Derek to do the honors, but I guess he won't mind under the circumstances."

After dinner, we both indulged in Tony's delicious cannoli. I definitely wouldn't have topped off dinner with dessert if my wedding dress hadn't fit perfectly when I last tried it on, just this morning. The bias cut of the gown made it brutally unforgiving, so I tried the dress on every day just to test the fit. I didn't want to gain an ounce before our wedding.

We lingered over dessert for a while. Despite consuming three cups of coffee, Wes stifled a yawn as he reached for the check.

"Am I keeping you up?" I teased.

He grinned. "Sorry. I hope the coffee will kick in soon. I'm going to be at the station until midnight at the rate I'm going."

"That's awful. Should we worry that you're not going to be able to go on our trip?"

"No way. I've already skipped too many vacations over the years. The captain agrees that Timmons can handle our cases while we're on our honeymoon."

Timmons had been Wes's partner for a few months now, and they'd established a good working relationship. After years of partnering with Felicia Smith, Wes had requested a change of partners when Felicia, who couldn't stand me, had told him that she loved him. Since Wes had never had any romantic feelings toward the abrasive, frizzy-haired detective, he'd been shocked, and he'd wanted to avoid having to work with her in the future. Although I'd been as surprised as Wes about Felicia's confession of love for him, I couldn't say I was sorry they were no longer partners since Felicia and I hadn't gotten along since the first time we'd met.

Wes had parked on the far side of the strip mall's lot under a big tree, so that his car would be in the shade while we had dinner. Once we'd passed a few rows of parked cars, the lot was empty, so we no longer had to weave our way in and out between parked vehicles. We were about thirty feet from the car when we heard a noise behind us. I turned and froze as I saw a large black pick-up truck headed straight toward us! My deer-in-the-headlights moment lasted just a split second, during which I literally couldn't move or make a sound.

Wes pushed me to the pavement and lay close beside me, his arm protectively draped over my shoulders. Miraculously, the truck passed right over us. Before the driver could turn his truck around, Wes pulled me up.

"Run!" he shouted as he grabbed my hand, and we dashed towards his car. We had such a momentum going that we had a difficult time stopping before we crashed into the side of the car.

The black truck had circled back and was coming at us again, but this time, we were able to get out of the way easily by scurrying to the other side of the car. Even then, I thought the driver might deliberately t-bone the car, and, this time, I did scream, but, at the last second, the driver veered off. Otherwise, he would have rammed the car, although, considering the size of his truck, its bumper would have absorbed most of the shock, and he probably wouldn't have been injured.

We watched as he revved the big black pick-up and peeled out of the parking lot. Wes hugged me close, and I clung to him fiercely. We stood there in a silent embrace for several seconds.

"Are you all right?" he asked finally. "I didn't want to push you down so hard, but I figured it was our only chance."

"Yes," I said, my voice trembling. "You saved our lives. When I saw that truck coming right at us, I couldn't move a muscle."

I looked down at myself to find that my knees and palms were scraped and bleeding. My sun dress had some grimy spots on it from the oily pavement, where my handbag and sweater still lay. Wes's suit had suffered similar damage.

"You're bleeding, sweetheart," he said. "Let's get you home so we can clean and bandage your cuts." He opened the passenger door, and I slid onto the seat, thankful to be alive and grateful to Wes for his quick action.

After he retrieved my handbag and sweater, Wes took out his cell phone and called in a report on the terrifying incident. I was still shaking from the ordeal and not really paying much attention to the conversation, but I heard him say something about the truck's mud-smeared license plates.

"I didn't even notice the license plates," I told him as he started the engine and adjusted the air conditioner. "Did you see something?"

"I couldn't see any numbers or even tell whether they were Iowa plates because they were caked with dirt, and I'm sure that was deliberate. I guess I don't need to tell you that whoever was driving that truck set out to get me. That's bad enough, but to involve you— that's pure evil." I hadn't put my seat belt on, and he gathered me into his arms. "I don't know what I'd do if anything ever happened to you."

"Oh, Wes," I sniffed, unable to prevent my tears from flowing. When I calmed down a bit, I asked him if he had any idea who the driver might be.

"Two or three people come to mind, all men I arrested, but, as far as I know, they're all still serving time. After we get you safely settled at home, I'm going to go back to the office to check on their status. In the meantime, the word's out to the troops to stop any vehicle that matches my description of the truck. I'm hoping we'll get lucky and find the guy this evening."

I shuddered to think that someone could hate Wes so much that he'd try to run him down.

When we reached home, Bear rushed me the instant Wes opened the door, and I hugged my furry canine companion with more fervor than usual, but he didn't seem to mind. As soon as I released him, he flopped down in front of Wes for his requisite tummy rub, which Wes didn't hesitate to give.

"You know, it's nice to be normal," he said, as Bear sat up, and he scratched behind his ears. "Sometimes we don't appreciate the everyday routine." He sighed. Wes didn't wax philosophical very often, so I knew the alarming incident had shaken him more than he'd let on.

Wes's cell phone rang, startling me, as I thought about how close we'd come to disaster just a few minutes ago.

"Wesson," he answered, and I could tell from his tone that it was official business.

"Right," he said. "I'll be there in five minutes." He turned to me. "We may have caught a break."

Chapter 3

"A patrol officer just made a traffic stop, a big black pick-up truck," he continued, "with muddy plates. Sounds like it may be our guy. I'm going over there to see if I can identify it."

"All right. I hope you can get him off the streets, if he's the one. Please call me as soon as you find out."

"I will. Are you sure you're all right?"

"Just some scrapes. I'll be fine. Good luck!"

After Wes left, I showered, dressed in a comfortable old t-shirt and robe, and put my green sun dress to soak in a cleaning solution in hopes of salvaging it. After I applied antiseptic to my scrapes, they didn't seem as bad as I'd feared at first, and I decided I didn't need to bandage them. I would definitely be bruised because we'd hit the parking lot pavement so hard. Luckily, my wedding gown would cover my bruised shins. If my hands still looked rough on our wedding day, I could always wear the fingerless lace gloves I'd purchased but later decided against wearing. I could take some maxi dresses on our honeymoon, instead of the shorter sun dresses I'd planned to take, and since I always wore pants, rather than shorts, in the summer because my fair skin burns so easily, I wouldn't have to change anything else in my honeymoon wardrobe.

Thinking about packing for the honeymoon briefly took my mind off the fact that someone had tried to kill us this evening, but it was difficult not to revisit what had happened. I kept seeing the truck bearing down on us and reliving the helpless feeling I'd had as I'd stared at it, unable to move.

To distract myself and pacify Bear, who, I could tell, sensed that something was wrong by the way he was pacing around my bedroom and whining softly, I took him outside and played a feeble game of fetch with him. He was soon panting because the temperature hadn't dropped much, so I sat in a lawn chair on the patio and called him to me. I petted him and talked soothingly to him for a few minutes, and he settled down at my feet on the cool flagstones. Soon he fell asleep, his legs mimicking running motions as he chased a rabbit or maybe a cat in his dreams.

I wanted to call Tracey to tell her about what had happened, but I'd left my smartphone inside, and I didn't want to wake Bear just yet. I sat there as the sky darkened, and I couldn't help thinking about my husband Tim's death in a car accident nearly six years ago. It had been sudden, so sudden he'd had no warning when a drunk driver hurtled from a side street and slammed into his car. And just like that, our life together was over. It had happened in an instant. It had happened once, and I was acutely aware that it could happen again. It could happen to Wes or me or both of us. That awful possibility made our time together very precious.

A ringing phone brought me out of my reverie. Bear heard it, too, and jumped up to go inside with me. My house phone was ringing. That was a bit unusual because everybody called me on my cell phone. I looked at the caller ID, expecting an unknown number, but it was Wes calling.

"Hi, sweetheart. I tried calling your cell, but when you didn't pick up, I thought I'd try your house phone."

"Oh, I must have left it in my handbag. Honestly, I

don't know where my head is."

"Never mind. We've both been through the mill this evening. How are you feeling?"

"I'm okay. Just a little jittery, I guess. I keep thinking we're lucky to be alive."

"Yes, we are, and I'm sorry I don't have better news to tell you now. I'm still at the scene of the traffic stop, but the truck the patrol officer stopped definitely isn't the one we're looking for. I knew it the minute I saw it because the hubcaps are totally different. The truck that almost ran us down in the parking lot had plain hubcaps, but this one has fancy custom wheel covers. The driver had been fishing and drove through some mud on a back road, so his plates are splattered, but they're not totally obscured like the ones on the truck we're looking for."

"Oh, no. I was hoping you'd catch the guy tonight."

"There's still a chance, but I don't think it's too likely. Whoever it is has had plenty of time to get off the streets and clean his plates. I'm going to head back to the office and check on a few likely perps. If any of them have been paroled, I can check their vehicle registrations."

"Will you let me know?"

"Of course. It may take some time, though."

"Why so long? I thought you said there might be just a couple of guys to check on."

"Well, I may have underestimated how many bear me a grudge. I'm going to do a thorough search of my files, and those go back several years."

"It sounds like you're going to be there all night. Maybe you should start fresh in the morning, instead."

I was almost positive that Wes wouldn't want to put his research off, but I hated to think he wouldn't get any sleep tonight and would have to work all day tomorrow.

I remembered that yawn at dinner, and I knew he was already tired, but, just as I'd thought, he was determined to go through his files right away. He told me he'd call me in the morning, and I had to be satisfied with that. When Wes made a decision, he seldom changed his mind.

I distracted myself by calling Tracey and filling her in on what had happened. She insisted on coming over, and since we both live in Hawkeye Haven, less than a mile apart, she showed up, armed with comfort snacks, in just a few minutes. Blond and bubbly, my cousin Tracey worked as an account executive for a Center City business. Despite her busy work schedule, she often took time for cooking and baking, both skills I'd never mastered, but I felt very happy she had because I could never turn down anything she made.

Bear trailed Tracey to the kitchen since he knew she never failed to bring him some homemade dog treats whenever she visited. She stooped to put a couple of treats in his bowl and gave him a gentle pat. As soon as he'd eaten them, he begged for more.

"Okay, Bear, just one more," she told the eager Lab. "Then it's mommy's turn."

"You brought me snacks, too?"

"Of course. Some comfort food will make you feel better."

"Very tempting, but I don't know if I should. We had a big dinner, and we both had dessert, too. I fit into my dress this morning, but I don't want to gain any weight right before the wedding. You know how clingy bias-cut dresses are."

"Have no fear. You can always diet tomorrow, if need be, but tonight you need to calm your nerves."

"Well, that's for sure. You've convinced me."

Tracey dished up some of her delicious mac and

cheese along with a piece of pumpkin cake with cream cheese frosting that looked scrumptious. She insisted on waiting on me.

"That's so good," I said, as I sampled the mac and cheese. "Aren't you having any?"

"I had just finished dinner when you called, but there's always room for dessert," she said, taking a bite of pumpkin cake. "My neighbor Kate Schoenherr gave me the recipe for the pumpkin cake. Try it; I know you'll like it just as much as I do."

"Umm. Absolutely delicious!"

"By the way, there's more if you want seconds."

"Oh, no. You gave me plenty. Thanks for coming over, Tracey. You really didn't have to. I'm doing all right."

"Don't be silly, Lo-lo," she said, calling me by my childhood pet name. "You could do with some company right now. I hope Wes can get to the bottom of this. You said he had an idea about who the driver might be."

I nodded. "At first, he mentioned that he could think of one or two men he'd put away, but when he called later, he said he planned to go through all his files. He's been a detective for fifteen years, so I'd say he has his work cut out for him."

"I'm so sorry this happened. Things have been going so smoothly lately, and you haven't run into any snags at all with your wedding plans. I just wish everything could be perfect for you and Wes. You two make a great couple."

"Thanks to you. I probably never would have gone out on that first date with Wes if you hadn't encouraged me. You even told me what to say, remember?"

"I remember it well. I could tell you really liked him, but you were having trouble *allowing* yourself to like him."

"I know. I suppose I felt disloyal to Tim in a way."

"I get it, but you know as well as I do that Tim wouldn't have wanted you to mourn forever. He'd want you to be happy."

"I know. It just took me a while to be able to do that. It helped a lot to move here. I'm glad you talked me into it."

"Me, too. Of course, I don't suppose our parents will ever stop trying to talk us into moving back to Seattle."

"Probably not, although I'm hoping mine will back off a little now that Wes and I are getting married. He can't very well leave his job here when he has over twenty years invested in it. I kind of wish he could do something that's not so dangerous, even though he says a detective's job is a lot safer than a beat cop's. If Wes were a teacher or an accountant, I doubt that someone would be trying to run him down."

Tracey stayed with me until almost midnight when I urged her to go home and get some sleep. I knew she had a busy schedule at work. After she left, I roused a sleepy Bear from his evening nap just long enough so that he could go into the bedroom and fall back asleep while I did the same.

Dawn came way too early, and it took me longer than usual to wake up while Bear panted, circled the bed, and nudged me with his nose. Finally, I gave in, and we went for our usual morning walk. After we got home, I brewed some strong coffee and took a mug with me to the patio while Bear lay beside me with an ear cocked for any move on my part that might signal it was time for his breakfast.

I was really curious about Wes's research of the night before, but I didn't want to call him in case he was sleeping. I knew he'd call me when he had a chance. It made me angry to think that a criminal blamed Wes for his predicament, but I realized that some people never took responsibility for their own actions.

I'd fed Bear, nibbled on some dry toast, and washed my green sun dress before Wes finally called.

"Did you get any sleep at all last night?" I asked.

"I did get a few hours, and I actually don't feel too bad," he assured me. "Plus, I think I may have a lead on our perp. As soon as I picked up his file, I remembered that he'd threatened the judge, the prosecutor, and me when the jury found him guilty of second-degree homicide. That was fourteen years ago. I checked, and he's out on parole. He's also the registered owner of a black pick-up truck. I'm just waiting to talk to his parole officer and find out where he's working. Then I'm going to pay him a visit."

"Oh, Wes, be careful!"

"Always, sweetheart. Don't worry. Timmons is going with me in case I need back-up, but I doubt that it'll come to that. If he is our guy, he's something of a coward to use his truck as a weapon."

"You'll let me know as soon as you talk to him? I'm really on pins and needles over this."

Wes promised me he'd let me know as soon as he discovered whether this suspect was the man who had tried to hit us, and I spent the morning on routine tasks while waiting for word. I didn't feel focused enough to work on my book, so I cleaned the kitchen and the bathroom, mopped the tile floors, and straightened and dusted until everything sparkled. Then I tackled my least favorite task—cleaning the glass patio sliders, which was double work because there was one in the den and another in the master bedroom. Bear followed me from room to room as I worked, except when I was vacuuming the bedroom carpets. I knew how much the noise bothered him, so I let him outside before I brought out the dreaded machine, and he never even saw it, although I knew he could hear it, even from the backyard.

By the time Wes called, I'd finished the chores and was happy to sit down. At least, I'd accomplished something, even though I hadn't written a word for *DIY Bridal Crafts*.

"Hi, sweetheart. I wish I had better news," Wes said.

My heart sank.

"I'm almost positive Michael Stanley isn't the guy. He was kind of a young punk when he was convicted, but I have to admit he seems like a changed man. If it's an act, he's convincing. He remembered me and actually apologized for the threats he made during his trial. He said nobody would hire him after his release from prison, so he borrowed some money from his mother and started his own lawn service. I caught up to him while he was mowing the lawn at the nursing home over on Fifth Street. I asked him how business was, and he said he couldn't complain. Then he handed his business cards to Timmons and me and asked us to keep him in mind if we ever needed lawn service."

"Well, he doesn't sound too suspicious, but what about the black truck?"

"He has one that he's using to haul a trailer with his equipment. The truck looked clean as a whistle. He must have washed it this morning. His trailer was just as clean, though."

"How did you find him?"

"I got his current address from his parole officer and went over to the house. He's living with his mother, who's retired, and she acts as a kind of dispatcher handling his calls for him. She told me where I could find him. She also said she was proud that he'd turned his life around. I think it would be hard to fool his own mother, so I tend to believe their stories."

"But you can't rule him out?"

"Not entirely, but it's time to look elsewhere. In the meantime, I've arranged to keep tabs on Michael."

"I don't suppose you're going to tell me how."

"I don't suppose so," he agreed.

"Honestly, Wes, sometimes you're the most maddening man!"

"Yup, and I'm madly in love with you."

Chapter 4

In the next few days, Wes wasn't able to identify any other viable suspects, and he concluded that the driver may have been a relative or friend of someone he'd sent to prison since there weren't any parolees, except Michael, living in Center City who might still hold a grudge against him. Thankfully, there were no more incidents.

Tracey was having a bridal shower for me Saturday afternoon at her house, and I was looking forward to celebrating my upcoming wedding with my friends. In the spirit of keeping it simple, the shower was the only pre-wedding event we had planned.

I selected a slinky maxi tank dress I'd made from rayon jersey and tie-dyed in shades of blue to wear to the shower. Blue is one of my favorite fashion colors because it looks good with my red hair. The blue dress did a nice job of covering up my bruised legs. I wouldn't be able to disguise the scrapes and bruises on my hands, but, by this time, all my friends had heard about what happened, and I wouldn't have to repeat the story again.

Tracey insisted that I bring Bear to the shower, too. Since my friends all liked Bear and I was sure he'd behave himself, I agreed. I'd even made him a cute blue bow tie that attached to his collar. I assured him that he was a handsome boy as he jumped into the back seat of my silver Honda SUV. It was a short distance to Tracey's house, and we could have easily walked, but

Tracey reminded me that I'd have gifts to bring home.

I felt a bit awkward about accepting shower gifts, especially since it wasn't as though Wes and I were starting our marriage without any furniture or household goods. We already had everything we needed. I'd suggested to Tracey that perhaps she could request no gifts on the shower invitations, but she wouldn't hear of it, claiming that presents were all part of the fun and that my friends wanted to give me gifts. I realized she was right after thinking about a couple of showers I'd attended for second-time brides in the past few years, so I didn't insist.

Bear and I were the first guests to arrive, since Tracey had asked me to come early. She exclaimed over Bear's bow tie, and my handsome Lab seemed to puff out his chest with pride. Tracey had decorated her living room with white paper wedding bells, baby blue candles, and white-and-blue floral arrangements.

"Tracey, everything looks beautiful! And fresh flowers, too? Those arrangements look fabulous, but complicated. However did you manage to find the time?" I knew her boss had insisted that her entire team work late the night before.

"I cannot tell a lie. Liz and Fran took care of the flowers, and they did a wonderful job. I'm so happy they volunteered to make your bouquet and all the flower arrangements for your wedding."

"So am I. A professional florist couldn't do a better job or have fresher flowers. They'll be picking them right from their own gardens, just a few hours before the wedding."

Tracey led me into the dining room where she'd arranged an equally beautiful table to set out the refreshments on later. I admired it while Bear followed her to the kitchen for a treat.

It wasn't long before Liz and Fran arrived, and I had a chance to thank them for arranging the lovely flowers. Striking in an orange beaded caftan and matching turban, eighty-year-old Liz wore huge gold hoop earrings and several gold rings on her fingers. Even Fran, our sixty-year-old neighbor, whose daily uniform consisted of old jeans, a t-shirt, and tennis shoes had dressed up a bit for the occasion in a long floral tunic, capris, and sandals. Wes's sister Denise arrived shortly after Liz and Fran, followed by Amy, Cynthia, Amber, Jennifer, and a few others who belonged to our book club but attended infrequently because their children often had activities scheduled on the weekends.

As the guests arrived, Tracey greeted them and placed the beautifully wrapped gifts they brought on a side table in the living room, where we all gathered. Tracey insisted I sit in a large armchair that she had decked out with blue and white streamers. Bear enjoyed the commotion as he sat next to me.

We played some frivolous shower games for a while, with Tracey keeping everything moving along at a nice pace, and soon we were all laughing at some of the silly questions we'd answered. As soon as each winner was announced, Tracey presented her with a large basket containing wrapped prizes and let her select one. Then she quickly went on to the next game.

For the last game, Tracey played several bars from a love song, and then we wrote the name of the song and who sang it on our game cards. Then we had to exchange cards with another guest to have our test scored. I was fairly hopeless at remembering song titles, and I recognized only a few of the singers, but Amy nailed it by correctly naming every song and singer. I wasn't surprised that Amy had won the game; after all, romance was practically her hobby. The petite widow loved to play matchmaker, listen to love songs, and read romance novels. We all clapped for her as she plucked her prize from the basket: fittingly, the latest romance novel from her favorite author.

Next Tracey invited me to open my presents. Bear got in the act each time I unwrapped one by putting his paw on my knee and looking it over. He was so cute that several guests pulled out their cell phones and took our picture. I knew Amber was sending some of the pictures to Alice already. Tracey hadn't been neglecting the photographs, either. She had her digital camera ready to capture every moment and snapped away with abandon. After I opened each gift and thanked the giver, Tracey returned it to the side table, making sure the card stayed with the gift.

Tracey excused herself to set up the buffet in the dining room, and Denise went along to help her. Bear, sensing an opportunity for a snack, followed. Soon Tracey returned and announced that refreshments were ready in the dining room. As we entered, we saw Denise pouring champagne into a huge punchbowl.

"There," she pronounced, giving it a quick stir. "Last, but not least."

The champagne punch was a pretty shade of light blue. Atop the punch, little molded rings of white and blue ice floated, as Denise ladled the punch into cut-glass cups that matched the punch bowl.

"That's a beautiful punch bowl," I said to Tracey. "I didn't know you had one."

"I don't. I borrowed the bowl, cups, and ladle from Liz and the glass plates, too. By the way, I gave Bear his treats out on the patio. He's wandering around the backyard now."

"Thanks, Tracey. I think we'll let him stay outside until everyone's had a chance to eat. There's plenty of shade, so he won't get too hot. He gets way too curious if any food's around."

Tracey insisted that I go first, and she'd prepared a scrumptious buffet: all sorts of little finger sandwiches, individual artichoke quiches, mini skewers with roasted beef tenderloin and pineapple, spicy deviled eggs, grape tomatoes, luscious strawberries, a tray of exotic cheeses, lemon cake pops, and white-and-blue meringues shaped like little flowers.

After I helped myself, I returned to my chair in the living room, covered my lap with a white linen napkin, and was pleased to find that the glass plate was easy to balance. The cup of champagne punch fit into a round raised glass rim on the plate that prevented the cup from sliding around. Since all the dishes Tracey had prepared were finger foods, we didn't need to balance any unwieldy utensils in our laps while we were eating.

Soon all the guests had returned to their spots in the living room and were chatting as they munched on the goodies. The noise level in the living room rose steadily as we talked. I noticed that Tracey had only a few items on her plate, and, after a while, she jumped up and circled the room, offering to replenish our plates or bring us more champagne punch. She'd brewed some coffee, too, but Liz and I were the only takers, besides Tracey herself.

Bear normally barked when he wanted to come in, but I hadn't heard him, and he'd been in the backyard quite a while, so I went to the kitchen and peeked out the window to check on him. He was sound asleep, lying on the grass, under a shady tree, so I left him to his nap and returned to the guests.

Jennifer was the only one there I hadn't seen lately. I pulled up a chair next to her so that we could catch up. She was now a wealthy woman, having inherited her husband's estate just a few months earlier, and, the last time I saw her, she was at loose ends, trying to decide what to do with the rest of her life. She'd talked about starting a design business, so I wondered whether she'd decided to take the plunge.

"Jennifer, I'm glad you're here. I haven't seen you for a while. How are your plans for the design business coming along?" I asked.

"Slowly. I want to do this right. My lawyers are working on the incorporation papers, and I've set up appointments to interview several key people Friday. I want to concentrate on the design part of the business and let other people handle the finances, manufacturing, and marketing"

"Wow! That sounds awesome." For some reason, I'd envisioned a little shop in downtown Center City, but it was obvious Jennifer had a much larger business in mind.

Jennifer smiled. "Yes. It's going to be bigger than I first imagined. I can afford to invest a substantial amount of money in this start-up, so I'm not going to hold back." She pulled her cell phone out of her handbag and tapped it. "Let me show you my new studio." She handed me the phone, and I couldn't help gaping at the photo of Jennifer's design studio, which looked like a feature in an upscale business magazine, with floor-to-ceiling windows and sleek, tasteful furnishings. "My goodness!" I exclaimed, "Your studio looks fantastic!"

Jennifer took the phone, flipped to a new picture, and handed it back to me. "Here's the view from the studio."

Obviously, Jennifer's studio was in a high-rise, and since there weren't many tall buildings in Center City, she must be planning to move.

"Chicago?" I guessed.

"That's right, and my parents are thrilled that I'm moving back. There's nothing holding me here now that Matt's gone, and Justin plans to transfer from Iowa State to Northwestern. It took me a while to figure out what I wanted to do, but I think I'm on the right track now. I'm sorry I haven't been in touch lately. I've been so busy with lawyers and meetings, and I was out of town for a few weeks."

I knew that Jennifer had felt stifled during her marriage and that she'd never worked outside the home. "No wonder we didn't see you at last week's book club meeting."

"Yes. I just returned a few days ago. I need to make arrangements to sell the house, and Tracey just mentioned to me that you and Wes are looking for a house, so you have first dibs, if you're interested."

"Thank you, Jennifer, but Wes insists that he doesn't want a two-story house. We're looking at a couple more places tomorrow, but we're not in a big hurry." What I didn't tell Jennifer was that not only was her house too big for Wes and me but also that I'd never be able to forget that her husband had been killed there. It was a lovely, huge house, but better suited to owners who had no bad memories of the place and better suited to a large family than a couple.

"I understand. In that case, I need to find a real estate agent so that I can list it. I guess there's not a huge rush, but I might as well get the ball rolling on the sale. Who are you working with?"

"Her name's Lisa Morrison, but we've been thinking about changing agents. She's very aggressive, and we don't want to be pushed into a deal that isn't right for us, just because she wants to sell a house. On the other hand, that trait might work in a seller's favor. I understand that she's the top salesperson at her agency, and they have more than twenty agents working there."

"Hmm. Well, she may be worth considering. I'll probably talk with two or three agents before I decide. You don't happen to have her card with you, do you?"

"I do, actually. Let me grab my purse, and I'll find it. Like I said, she may be too high-powered for us, but that might be good for you." I found my little clutch bag tucked behind a pillow in the chair where I'd been sitting, pulled Lisa's card out of my wallet, and handed it to Jennifer.

"Thanks, Laurel. I think I'll give her a call as soon as I get one or two more recommendations from other people. I'm really sorry I won't be here for the wedding. If you have time this week, let's get together for lunch. Maybe Amy and Cynthia could join us."

"That would be nice."

"Not too much for you? I know you're probably swamped with wedding planning."

"Not really. We have everything arranged, and so far, there haven't been any glitches. Probably early in the week would work best for me, though, because my parents will be arriving on Thursday."

"All right. Let's check with Amy and Cynthia."

Just as I was about to get up, Bear began barking frantically. I could tell his little nuances, and this sounded like more than just wanting to come back inside the house. I excused myself and went to the kitchen door. He had his front paws braced on the door, but he backed down as soon as he saw me coming and raced inside when I opened the door. Oddly, he didn't even pause in the kitchen, where extra food was laid out on the counter tops.

"Bear, come here," I called, and he turned and ran back to me, but then took off again.

Tracey was about to open the front door when she saw Bear coming. "Just a delivery," she said. "Probably the sandals I ordered online." Tracey bought almost everything, except her groceries, online, so she was constantly getting packages delivered.

I went over to the door and held Bear by his collar, tipping his blue bow tie to a sporty angle, while Tracey opened the door.

At the sight of the skinny, long-haired young man, dressed in a gray short-sleeved shirt and matching pants, Bear snarled and growled, and the man hastily handed Tracey a package and beat a quick retreat while Bear barked furiously.

"That's odd," I said as Tracey closed the door. "Bear usually barks when I get a delivery, but he's never acted like that before when someone came to the door."

"Maybe he didn't like the guy," Tracey said. "He looked sort of sketchy to me. I'm just going to put this in the bedroom, and I'll be right back."

The guests had all watched Bear's performance in surprise, but, now that he'd settled down, they complimented him on being a good watch dog. It was a wonder he hadn't knocked someone over in his frenzied dash to the front door. I straightened his bow tie, and told him to sit as I joined Amy and Cynthia, who were talking to Jennifer now.

"What a cute bow tie!" Amy said. "Is he going to wear it to the wedding?"

"How did you guess?" I chuckled. "Tracey suggested that he could be the ring bearer, but I thought that would be taking things too far."

Bear basked in the attention as we arranged our lunch date for noon Monday at Alberto's. Since we all live in Hawkeye Haven, and the restaurant was right next to the community center, we figured it would be the easiest place to meet. Even though Cynthia was serving as the interim director for Food for Families, she maintained a flexible schedule and hadn't been planning to work that day, so she wouldn't have to rush back to work.

"I wasn't going to mention this now, and I've already told Amy, but I think you both probably need to know," Cynthia said, looking at me and Jennifer. "I bet you'll be as shocked as I am."

"What is it?" Jennifer asked.

"It's Marcie," Cynthia said. "She's back in town. I saw her leaving Foster's when I was grocery shopping there this morning. I was in the check-out line, and I called to her, but either she didn't hear me, or she was ignoring me."

"Well, I admit I *am* shocked," I said. "I wouldn't have thought she'd have the nerve to come back to Center City after what she did." Marcie, the former director of Food for Families, had embezzled a substantial amount of money from the nonprofit, charitable organization. Both Amy and I, along with the FFF's other board members, had had the unenviable task of confronting Marcie with the evidence of her crime. We'd sought to set up a plan for her to repay the money she'd stolen, but she'd stormed out of the board meeting before she'd even heard the details of our proposal, and nobody had seen her since.

"Isn't there a warrant out for her arrest?" Jennifer asked. Although Jennifer wasn't an FFF board member, her late husband Matt had been on the board and had left a generous donation to the organization, contingent on an audit, which he'd designated me to supervise. The audit had uncovered Marcie's embezzlement.

"Yes," Amy said. "When she wouldn't cooperate with us and then just disappeared, the board decided to go to the district attorney. She could be arrested at any moment, but if that happens, the publicity won't be good for FFF."

"That's for sure," I said.

"Girls! Girls!" Tracey announced, and the chatter ceased as all the guests turned their attention to her. "We have one final game before we wrap up with the grand prize yet to give away. The lucky winner gets a gift card for the Pizza Palace and two movie tickets," she said, as she distributed game cards. "Everybody have your pens?"

"Just a second. I need to find mine," Liz said, as she dug into her huge handbag. "Ah, here it is."

"Okay. Good. This is an easy one, and Liz already has the right idea because what you're going to do is make a check mark on your game card for each item listed that you can find in your purse. If you have something in your purse that's not listed, it doesn't count for any points. Otherwise, you can see how many points each item is worth on your card. Take five or ten minutes to fill out your card, and then add up the points. Whoever has the most points wins."

"What if we have two of the same thing, Tracey?" Fran asked. "Do we count them twice?"

"Good question. Only count them once. Like if you have five coins or two combs, you just get credit for one coin and one comb."

We began checking off wallets, keys, lipsticks, combs, tissues, cash, and the many other items we had in our handbags that were on the game card Tracey had given us. I'd brought a small clutch with me, so I had far fewer items than usual. I finished filling out my card in a few minutes, and, when I totaled my check marks, they amounted to a measly thirty points.

Others were still sorting and adding up their points,

though, and it was a few minutes before Tracey called the game to a halt and asked us to exchange cards to double-check our math. Then she collected the cards and quickly found the winner.

It came as no surprise to me that Liz won the game. After all, she had the largest bag, and it was stuffed with all kinds of essentials. Liz always carried lots of makeup and her e-reader. Today, she also had a large-print paperback novel, worth a whopping fifty points.

"Liz, how much does that bag weigh?" Amber teased. "I thought my bag was packed until I saw yours."

"I like to have everything I need with me," Liz said. "You wouldn't believe how handy it is when I'm under the dryer at the beauty parlor or waiting at a doctor's office."

"I hope the colonel likes pizza," Tracey said, as she handed Liz her gift card and voucher for movie tickets.

"He does, and he's been wanting to see that new action thriller," Liz said, tucking the prizes into her purse.

"Now don't lose those in there," Fran cautioned with a smile.

After the game was over, the guests departed, and Tracey and I relaxed with another cup of coffee. Tracey had been so busy as hostess that she'd barely had a bite to eat, so she snagged several sandwiches and the two remaining deviled eggs.

"Mmm. Not bad," she said, munching on a cream-cheese-and-cucumber finger sandwich.

"Are you kidding?" I said. "Everything was absolutely delicious!"

"Thanks, Lo-lo. It was fun."

Bear had been lying beside me, snoozing. Suddenly, he raised his head and looked toward the front door. He jumped up and stood at the door, tail wagging.

"He must hear somebody coming," I said.

"Obviously, it's not our weird delivery guy," Tracey replied before the doorbell rang.

"I'll get it," I told Tracey.

As soon as I opened the door, I knew Bear had been wagging his tail because our visitor was Wes. We managed a hug before Bear claimed Wes's attention with his usual antics.

"I thought you might need some help," Wes said, "to take all your loot home."

"You mean *our* loot?"

"That's right." He planted a big kiss on my lips. "*Our* loot."

"Seriously, we received some lovely gifts, and I'm going to write thank-you notes for all the shower presents right away and get them in the mail. You'll write half the thank-yous for the wedding gifts, right?"

"Uh."

When Tracey and I saw the look of distress on Wes's face, we burst out laughing.

"Don't worry. I'm just kidding. I'll take care of those, too."

"Oh, good. That's a relief."

"How about a snack, Wes?" Tracey suggested. "I'm out of deviled eggs, but there's plenty of other food left. Just help yourself."

"I'll get you some coffee," I volunteered, "unless you'd rather have champagne punch."

"Coffee would be great," Wes said, following me to the kitchen to wash his hands before he surveyed the left-overs on the dining room table and loaded a plate with snacks.

We all talked for a while before Tracey asked Wes to help her put some bedding on the top shelf in her closet.

Bear got up, and I thought he would follow them, but he went to the kitchen door, so I let him outside.

I could hear Tracey and Wes talking, and their tone sounded serious. My radar alerted, I joined them in Tracey's bedroom, where I could see them staring at the package that had arrived earlier, now open on the bed.

"What's going on?"

"Oh, Lo-lo. I didn't want you to know about this," Tracey said as I looked at the contents of the box.

Chapter 5

"Dead roses," I said. "What in the world?"

"Black, too," Tracey said glumly. "I didn't want to say anything to you. I wanted your shower to be perfect."

"It was perfect," I said, slipping my arm around her shoulder. "What's this all about?" I looked at Wes questioningly.

"Tracey thinks her ex-boyfriend sent the package."

"Not Liam Murphy?" Tracey had dated Liam for a while a year ago, but he'd moved to Florida when he was transferred. She'd had lots of dates since then, but there was nobody special in her life. Despite its high-pressure intensity, she loved her job and didn't seem interested in a permanent relationship.

"I don't know of anybody else who would pull a stunt like this. I admit it upset me, so I guess he accomplished his goal. He's been practically stalking me ever since he came back to Center City last month."

"Why didn't you tell me?" I burst out. We had confided in each other our entire lives.

"With the wedding coming up, I didn't want to worry you, and, honestly, I don't think he's really dangerous. He just won't take 'no' for an answer."

"Tracey, could you please bring me a paper towel and a small trash bag?" Wes asked.

"Sure."

"You're keeping it as evidence?" I asked when Tracey had left the room.

"Yup. Just a precaution. I doubt that we'll need it, but it's better to open a case file now and preserve the evidence."

"Case file?" Tracey looked alarmed as she popped back in, plastic bag and paper towel in hand. "But I don't want to get Liam into any trouble. I only want him to stop pestering me."

"I understand, and that's what I'm hoping to achieve." Wes repeated what he'd told me about preserving evidence. "I think it's about time I paid a call on Mr. Murphy, before his behavior escalates," Wes said. "Do you know where he's living?"

"Some apartment complex over on Cedar Street, but I have no idea which one. He's back working at St. Anne's Hospital."

"Doctor?"

"No, he's a manager in the accounting department."

"I'm going to see what I can find out. Why don't you stay here until I come back, and then I'll take you both out for a nice dinner."

I could tell Tracey was ready to protest, but I caught her eye and shook my head. I knew that when Wes decided to take action, there was no stopping him. I also knew better than to try. "It sounds like a plan," I said, kissing him good-bye. After Wes left, I urged Tracey to come outside with Bear and me.

"Okay," she agreed. "Let me find his rubber ball, and we'll play fetch with him for a while."

We'd just wrapped up our game, and a panting Bear was lying on the cool kitchen floor when Wes called to say that he'd lucked into dinner reservations for eight-thirty at a popular steakhouse because there'd been a cancellation. So far, he hadn't been able to contact Liam in person, and even though Tracey had given Wes his cell phone number, he didn't want to call and alert

Liam that he was looking for him. Wes always said he could get a better feel for whether or not a person was lying or telling the truth by an in-person meeting.

"Let's pack up the presents and take them to my house," I said. "Wes can pick us up there. Anyway, it's past time for Bear's dinner. He'd be begging for sure if we hadn't worn him out playing fetch."

It didn't take long for us to stow the gifts in the back of my SUV, and Bear perked up when he realized we were headed for home and his dinner. I texted Wes to let him know that he could pick us up at my house, rather than Tracey's.

Wes arrived with only a few minutes to spare until the time of our reservation, and he whisked us off, just in the nick. Our table awaited us. After all the goodies I'd consumed at the shower, I wasn't very hungry, so I ordered a small steak salad, while Tracey selected a petite fillet, and Wes decided on a t-bone. The place was packed, and the noise level so high that we had to raise our voices to communicate. It didn't help that background music blared from hidden speakers, so we didn't linger after dinner.

"Sorry it was so loud in there," Wes said, as he opened the back door for Tracey. "I can't complain about my steak, though. It was excellent."

"Mine, too," Tracey said. "They really do have the best steaks in town. Thank you for treating."

"My pleasure."

On the way to Tracey's house, Wes finally told us what he'd learned.

"I tracked down Liam's address, and I went over to his apartment. He wasn't home, but don't worry. I'll catch up with him."

"Wes, do you really think it's necessary to talk to him?" Tracey sounded worried.

"I do, and I'll keep you posted. In the meantime, don't answer his calls or respond to his texts. And don't answer your door unless you know who it is."

"Okay. I won't, but now you're scaring me."

"I'm not trying to. Just be cautious. I know all the residents in Hawkeye Haven think they're safe, and you're probably safer at home than elsewhere, but the guards and walls are no guarantee that someone can't get in who doesn't belong. Your delivery man, for example. I checked with Luke, and nobody fitting the description of the guy was admitted at either gate this afternoon."

Luke, Liz's grandson, was Hawkeye Haven's head of security, so he supervised the gate guards and drivers of the rover who patrolled Hawkeye Haven twenty-four hours a day, seven days a week.

"Luke also said none of the regular postal or delivery service vehicles entered then, either, so the guy must have come over the wall to gain entry."

"I thought he looked sketchy," Tracey declared. "Very weird. I can't imagine Liam going to all the trouble of hiring some guy to sneak into Hawkeye Haven to deliver a package."

"Curiouser and curiouser," I said, perplexed.

Chapter 6

"I still haven't made contact with Liam, and I've tried a couple times, both late last night and this morning," Wes told me. "Could be he's out of town for the weekend, or I'm just missing him. He should be at work in the morning, though, so I'll go over there first thing, before I go into the office. I still want a face-to-face with him."

"It's hard for me to picture him as a stalker," I said. "He always used to joke around, and he seemed kind of goofy. I think Tracey thought that he was fun at first, but by the time he was transferred, I think his immaturity had worn thin, as far as she was concerned."

"He may think of himself as a prankster, but he needs to understand that he could get himself into some serious trouble if he keeps harassing Tracey. She could get a restraining order, if need be, but maybe we can nip this problem in the bud."

"I hope so," I said fervently.

Wes and I were on our way to another round of home tours. Lisa had added a couple more properties to the list, and she had asked us to meet her at the real estate office, so that we could all go together in her car. Of course, if we did that, she'd be in the driver's seat, both literally and figuratively. It was another of her tactics to keep control, but I wasn't buying it this time. I'd texted her to let her know we'd meet her at the first house. She didn't give up easily and hadn't supplied us with its address until a few minutes before we were scheduled to look at the house.

As Wes drove, I glanced again at the pictures I'd printed of the houses we were going to see. I'd allowed myself the tiniest bit of excitement because a couple of them looked fabulous in their pictures. As usual, every property on the list was priced above our targeted number, but Lisa insisted that we could always negotiate the price.

"Turn left onto Fairway?" Wes asked.

"Yes, and then take the first right on Maquoketa. It's about four blocks down the street, number 2132."

"Beautiful neighborhood."

"It sure is. I have a feeling this one's going to be a budget-buster, though. Just look at how big these yards are."

"Here we are," Wes said, parking in front of number 2132. "I don't see Lisa's BMW. Maybe we beat her to it. Let's look around the yard while we wait for her."

"I don't know if we should," I said hesitantly. "There's a car in the driveway. The owners must be home."

"No. This one's vacant, remember?"

"Oh, right. I see a lock box next to the doorbell. Maybe Lisa's driving a different car."

"Could be."

Stopping to admire some of the plants in the front yard, we strolled leisurely to the front door. It wasn't open, and Lisa didn't answer the doorbell, so Wes suggested we look at the backyard while we waited for her. We followed the sidewalk around the house to the back patio. Even though the backyard was enclosed with an ugly chain-link fence, the gate wasn't locked. In the center of the backyard, we saw a large pool. The yard sloped downhill beyond the pool, which would have looked as though it went on forever, if there weren't a wooded area in back of the house beyond the pool.

But there was something besides the stunning optical illusion of the infinity pool that caught my eye. Someone was in the pool, and she was no swimmer.

"Wes!" I shouted. "Look! In the pool!"

A woman floated face down in the calm water, her long, bright burgundy hair fanning out around her head. It was immediately obvious that she wasn't swimming. She wore a navy skirt suit, not a swim suit.

Wes had seen her at the same time I had, and he flipped his sandals aside as he ran toward the pool. "Call an ambulance!" he yelled as he jumped in.

I pulled my smartphone from my purse and dialed 9-1-1. There was a maddening delay when I told the operator it was a medical emergency, and I had to wait for a different dispatcher. Although the wait probably lasted only a few seconds, it seemed longer.

With the rescue unit on the way, I rushed to the edge of the pool. Wes had towed the woman to the side, and I helped him maneuver her onto the patio. She still had shoes on her feet—six-inch black stiletto platforms. The shoes didn't register until Wes rolled her onto her back and I recognized Patty Morrison, the former manager of Hawkeye Haven's HOA. She'd dyed her hair, but it was Patty, all right. I'd even seen her wear these same shoes before.

"It's Patty Morrison!"

"She's not breathing," Wes said after he'd put his ear to her mouth. He grabbed her wrist and felt for a pulse.

"No pulse." Immediately, he started CPR while I watched, feeling helpless.

"I'll signal the rescue unit," I told him as soon as I heard sirens. I ran to the front of the property, and, when I saw the unit approaching, I signaled them.

"Around back," I told them, leading the way.

One of the men took over CPR from Wes, and Wes and I stepped back. Another siren sounded, and two patrol officers appeared on the scene. One of them, an officer who looked so young I would have thought he was a high school student if he hadn't been in uniform, called Wes "lieutenant."

"I'll give you the details of what happened here for your report in just a minute, Atkins," Wes told him.

"Is she alive, lieutenant?" the young cop asked.

"I don't know. I wasn't having any luck with CPR, but maybe the rescue squad can revive her. Excuse me, just one second. I need to make a quick call."

I handed Wes my smartphone. Fortunately, he'd left his cell phone in the car. If he'd had it in his pocket as usual, it would be water-logged now.

He walked to the far side of the patio and had a quick conversation before returning to us.

"This is a suspicious drowning, so detectives have been assigned to investigate," he told the patrol officers.

"Can't you investigate, lieutenant?" the young officer asked, ignoring his partner who nudged him.

"The case has been assigned to Walker and Smith," Wes told them. He didn't elaborate, but he'd already told me that his partner Timmons would handle their ongoing cases while Wes was on vacation, and the captain had decided to assign any new cases to other detectives until after Wes returned from our honeymoon.

In the meantime, the rescue crew worked nonstop to revive Patty. They stopped the CPR and placed an oxygen mask over her face.

"We're ready to transport," one of the crew members said.

"Which hospital?" the young patrolman's partner

asked.

"St. Anne's."

The paramedics secured Patty on a portable gurney and wheeled her to the waiting rescue unit.

"Should we go to St. Anne's?" the rookie asked Wes, but his partner answered him and told him they should stay where they were until Lieutenant Walker arrived.

Wes's wet shirt and shorts clung to him and water dripped down his arms and legs. While we waited for Walker to arrive, I found a ragged old towel Wes kept in his trunk in case of an emergency, and he dried himself as best he could.

Just as he flung the wet towel around his shoulders, Walker showed up, dressed as casually as Wes.

"Never fails. Always on a weekend, huh, Wesson?" Walker grumbled.

"Seems like it," Wes agreed.

"What do we have?"

As Wes brought Walker up to speed, I found a shady spot on a little bench under a huge tree on the side of the patio. I looked out at the placid water in the infinity pool. Calm and inviting though the water looked, it had been the scene of a tragedy just a few minutes earlier. I wondered why Patty had been at the house, how she'd come to be in the pool, and why Wes thought her death hadn't been an accident. Even though he always played it close to the vest when he investigated a case, I felt sure he'd tell me the reason he had suspicions since he was a witness in this case, rather than an investigator.

Where was Lisa? She should have met us by now. I supposed we'd been at the house for close to an hour at this point. I looked at my smartphone to check the time and noticed that I had a text message I hadn't checked yet. Sure enough, it was from Lisa, saying she'd had an offer to write up for one of the buyers she'd been working with, and another agent would meet us at 2132 Maquoketa.

Patty had owned her own property management company when she'd managed Hawkeye Haven's HOA. I didn't know whether her company still existed, but she must be a real estate agent, the same agent covering for Lisa. Then it dawned on me that they had the same last name. Were they related?

I decided I should find out before I told Lisa that Patty had almost drowned and had been taken to St. Anne's. I called the real estate office and spoke to another agent, who confirmed that Patty was working for the agency and that Lisa was her sister.

I tried to call Lisa, but my call went straight to voice mail, so I sent her a text saying it was urgent that she contact me immediately. Within a minute, she returned my call.

"Laurel, I'm right in the middle of negotiating a deal, but I can juggle it if you've decided to put in an offer."

"No offer—" I didn't have a chance to tell her the reason I was calling before she interrupted me.

"I don't really have time right now. Check with me later."

"Wait!" I said urgently. "This is an emergency!"

I guess my tone grabbed her attention because she asked me what was so important.

"It's about Patty."

"Don't tell me she didn't meet you to show you the house."

"Yes. She was here."

"Well, then, you can speak to her about any questions you have," she said impatiently. "She's a licensed agent."

"There's been an accident," I blurted. "Patty's been taken to St. Anne's. We found her in the pool."

"What? Why didn't you say so? Is she all right?"

"She wasn't breathing when Wes pulled her out of the pool, but she's been given CPR, and the paramedics put her on oxygen before they left. It looked like she was still unconscious."

"Of all the harebrained stunts she's pulled, this takes the cake. I bet she tripped in those ridiculous shoes of hers." She started to say something else, but stopped herself, perhaps realizing how she must be coming across to a prospective client. "Uh, thanks for letting me know, Laurel. I'll check the hospital. Oh, and would you like me to send out another agent so you and Wes can look at the other houses? You must be at the Maquoketa house, right? It's the only one on your schedule for today with a pool."

"I think we're done for today, Lisa. I hope Patty's all right."

I could hear voices in the background as Lisa talked to other people before saying "gotta go" and hanging up abruptly.

That was odd, I thought, as I dropped my cell phone into my handbag. I didn't have a sister, but Tracey, my cousin and BFF, was as close to me as any sister could be, and I knew if I'd received an urgent phone call like the one I had just made to Lisa, I would have been on my way to the hospital as soon as I heard the news. Lisa seemed more concerned about closing her deal and retaining Wes and me as her clients than she did about her own sister. I didn't know whether or not she intended to visit St. Anne's anytime soon, but I certainly did, and I knew Wes would want to check on Patty's condition, too. It wasn't every day that we found a drowning victim in a swimming pool and Wes had to perform CPR.

Wes and Walker broke off their conversation at the

arrival of Sergeant Felicia Smith, Wes's former partner. Smith looked different from the last time I'd seen her. At first, I thought she'd straightened her hair, but it was so long that I realized she must be wearing a wig. She was wearing heavy make-up, too, but it wasn't enough to conceal the redness of her skin. She had a terrible sunburn. She wore a short, shapeless dress with no sleeves, and I could see that her arms and legs were sunburned, too. Or maybe she'd stayed in a tanning bed far too long. Her long, dangle earrings and her silver link bracelet, loaded with charms, looked out of place, under the circumstances.

The last time I'd seen Smith, months ago, she'd been excruciatingly polite to me, but she didn't bother this time. She spotted me sitting on the bench before she joined Wes and Walker.

"You *would* be here," she said sarcastically, but not loudly enough so that Wes could hear. I ignored her. She hadn't liked me since the first time we'd met when Bear deposited some of his brown fur on her white linen pants. Things had gone downhill from there.

As soon as she reached Wes, Walker, and the patrolmen, Wes left, acknowledging her with just a brief nod.

"Let's go, sweetheart," he said. "I'd like to put on some dry clothes."

"Then we can go to the hospital to check on Patty."

"My thoughts exactly," he agreed. "I figured you'd want to find out how she's doing."

"Yes. I found out that Lisa's her sister, so I called to let her know what happened." I filled Wes in on the conversation I'd had with Lisa as we drove to his apartment. Although he agreed that her reaction was strange, he cautioned me not to read too much into it since people don't always react to bad news the way we'd expect.

"I'll just be a few minutes," Wes told me as he unlocked his apartment door. "I smell like chlorine, so I need to take a shower, but I promise I'll make it quick."

"Okay. I'll pack a few books while I'm waiting."

Wes had been fortunate to find a sub-lessor for his apartment, especially since his lease had five more months to run. He'd lived in the third-story, two-bedroom apartment for years, but you'd never know it from the sparse furnishings, which he was giving to the young teacher who was taking over the lease. He'd just graduated from college, Wes had told me, and would be teaching summer school before starting the regular fall term, but he had more student loans than cash on hand, and he was glad to be able to rent a furnished apartment.

Wes would have to move only his clothing, a few personal items, and his extensive book collection. He had lots of hardback books, mainly history and biography. I could see that, although he'd begun packing them in sturdy boxes, he hadn't gotten too far. Each box was flat and was assembled by folding it into place. I put one together, and carefully packed it with several books. Then I assembled the lid and popped it on the box. I lifted the box and found it was quite heavy. By the time I packed another box, Wes had changed into dry clothes.

"These boxes are really heavy, Wes."

Wes piled one box on top of another and made lifting them look easy. "Not so bad." He grinned. "I take it you don't want to move them."

"Very funny, Mr. Muscles," I replied. My routine lifting five-pound weights may have toned my arms, but I wasn't about to volunteer for this mission. "I'll help you unpack them," I conceded.

"It's a deal," he said, as he gestured toward the door. "Shall we?"

Predictably, the parking lot at St. Anne's was packed, and Wes had to park on the far side of the lot. I supposed that Sunday afternoon must be prime visiting time at the hospital.

Parking so far away from the entrance reminded me of our close call the last time we parked in a lot, but the aisles were so narrow, and the parked cars were jammed so close together that it would have been impossible to pull the same stunt here.

We headed toward the emergency room, where Wes spoke with the receptionist. I noticed he pulled out his badge and ID before approaching her. "I'm going in the back to speak with the doctor," Wes told me. "I won't be long."

I nodded, knowing that the only reason Wes was buzzed through the locked door was that he was a police officer. If I'd been a relative, I could have gone with him, but, as it was, I'd have to cool my heels in the waiting room until he returned with news.

In fifteen minutes, he was back.

"How is she?" I asked.

"She still hasn't regained consciousness. I spoke to the doctor, and she said it was too soon to make a prognosis. There's a uniformed officer back there to keep an eye on her."

"You never did tell me why you suspect foul play."

"There was a ugly gash around her neck."

I hadn't noticed any mark on her throat when I'd helped Wes get Patty out of the pool, but I'd been concentrating on trying to pull her onto the patio while Wes lifted her body.

"I think someone strangled her with her own necklace and then pushed her into the pool. Whoever did it probably thought she was already dead."

"That's awful. Do you suppose someone followed her there? I mean how would anyone know she was going to be at that particular house? We didn't even know it."

"You think someone targeted Patty?"

"Well, she certainly wasn't very popular, especially among Hawkeye Haven residents, but I can't imagine any of them would still be so angry with her that they'd attack her. She hasn't been the HOA manager there for several months, anyway."

"Could be she made some enemies since then."

"Knowing Patty, I don't doubt it."

"What's that? You *know* Patty?" I heard the voice behind me and turned to find Lisa standing there.

Chapter 7

"I live in Hawkeye Haven, remember?"

"Oh, right, of course." Lisa seemed distracted. Her phone rang and, she removed herself to a corner of the waiting room, where she plucked it from her pocket and held an animated five-minute conversation.

Wes and I looked at each other in disbelief. She hadn't even asked how Patty was doing yet.

"I only have a few minutes," she said when she came back. "I have to take a contract to some sellers for their signatures, but I thought I'd run by here on the way. Do you know which room Patty's in?"

"She's still in the emergency room," Wes told her, "and she's still unconscious. The doctor told me they'll be transferring her to the ICU soon."

"Oh, well, I guess there's nothing I can do here, then," she said. "I'll see you later."

Wes and I were both so stunned that we didn't react right away.

"Unbelievable! Do you think she understands how serious this is?" I asked Wes. "She didn't even ask to see Patty."

"No, she didn't," he said thoughtfully. "I'll make sure to tell Walker about her reaction."

"You don't really think she tried to strangle her own sister, do you?"

"Stranger things have happened. We always look at the family when there's a suspicious death, so Walker or Smith will be interviewing her in any case."

"Speaking of family—"

A girl wearing a frilly peasant blouse, jeans, and flip-flops was coming through the sliding glass doors at the emergency room's entrance. She looked around in confusion. When she saw me, she approached us timidly.

"Hi, Laurel. I don't know if you remember me. I came to your class the other day with Tara." She made it sound like a question, rather than a statement.

"Of course, I remember you, Megan. This is Wes, my fiancé."

"My mom's here," she said, her voice quavering.

"We know. They're taking care of her. I'm afraid she's still unconscious."

"Can I see her?"

"Sure. I'll take care of it," Wes said, before going to the reception desk.

"They'll buzz you in, right over there," Wes told her, indicating the door.

"Could you come with me?" she asked me. She looked terrified, and I shot a help-me glance at Wes.

"We'll all go," he said, moving toward the door.

The buzzer sounded as we approached the door, and the receptionist turned away, so she never noticed that I'd accompanied Wes and Megan into the emergency room. It was probably a good thing I was there, though. Megan was clutching my arm so hard that I could feel her nails digging into it. Wes showed us the way and nodded to the uniformed officer standing outside the small cubicle where Patty lay.

"There's no change in her condition," a woman in a white coat told Wes, as soon as we came in.

"Dr. Schepman, this is Patty's daughter Megan," he told her.

"Your mother's unconscious, Megan. We're hoping

she'll regain consciousness soon."

"Is she going to die?" Megan whispered.

"It's possible," the doctor said. Seeing Megan's face crumple, she added, "I wish I had better news for you, but we just don't know. We'll move her to the ICU in just a minute and monitor her there. It's on the third floor if you want to go on up and wait for her there."

Megan burst into tears. I put my arm around her and led her out of the cubicle, into the hallway.

"Let's go upstairs," I suggested to her. She sniffed and bobbed her head slightly.

Although there was an elevator at the end of the hall in the emergency room, it was strictly reserved for hospital personnel, so we returned to the waiting room in search of the public elevator.

I'd just spotted the sign with an arrow pointing the way to the elevators when Tara rushed in and made a beeline for Megan. The minute Megan saw her, she began to sob again. Tara put her arms around her and let her cry on her shoulder until she was alternately hiccuping and gasping for breath. Then Tara urged Megan to sit down. She sat beside her and handed her a wad of tissues.

"Would you like some water, Megan?" I asked, but she shook her head.

"Oh, hi, Laurel," Tara greeted me. "Sorry I didn't even see you when I came in."

She shook hands with Wes as I introduced them. I explained the situation briefly, and she offered to accompany Megan to the ICU and to stay with her until her aunt returned.

I drew Tara aside and quietly told her that Lisa had already been here, but she'd left without seeing her sister. "I don't know whether she's planning on coming back later or not," I told her.

"From what Megan's told me, Lisa's laser-focused on her business. Megan seems to accept that, but I don't think she gets much more attention from her aunt than from her mother."

"You're a good friend to her, and from the sound of it, she certainly needs one."

"She does, and don't worry: I'll stay with Megan as long as she needs me, whether Lisa shows up or not."

Megan had dried her tears by this time.

"Come on, Megan. Let's go upstairs to the ICU now," Tara suggested, and Megan meekly followed her toward the elevator.

"Poor kid," Wes commented as we exited the emergency room.

He took my hand as we turned right, toward the parking lot. Head down, a man was slowly walking toward us, his eyes glued to his cell phone. He didn't notice us as he walked by and brushed against my purse, knocking it to the ground.

"Oh. I'm sorry," he apologized as he stopped to pick up the bag for me. "I didn't see you."

I didn't recognize him until he stood and handed me my purse. "Liam?"

Chapter 8

"Laurel McMillan!" Liam exclaimed as he planted a quick kiss on my cheek while Wes glowered at him. "Long time, no see."

"This is my fiancé, Wes," I told Liam.

"Liam Murphy?" Wes asked.

"That's right. You must have heard of me." Liam grinned in his happy-go-lucky way.

"Oh, I've heard of you, all right," Wes said, flashing his badge. "Detective Lieutenant Wesson, Center City Police Department," he stated matter-of-factly.

"Whoa!" Liam turned to me. "You're engaged to a *cop*?"

Wes ignored Liam's question to me and posed one of his own. "Did you send flowers to Tracey yesterday?"

"No, I haven't sent her any flowers for a couple of weeks. Why? What's this all about?" Liam looked genuinely perplexed.

"She says you've been harassing her."

"Asking a girl for a date is hardly harassment."

"It is if you keep asking after she's told you she's not interested."

"Oh, give me a break. That's persistence, not harassment. I know she really wants to go out with me. She just likes to play games."

"No, she doesn't, Liam," I interjected, against my better judgment.

"She's told me, in no uncertain terms, that your attention is not welcome, Murphy," Wes said. "That's a fact. Stop trying to contact the lady. If you keep it up, she'll be forced to get a restraining order, and the hospital might not take it too kindly."

"Oh, man. You haven't talked to my boss, have you?"

"Not yet."

"Well, don't! He's had it in for me ever since I came back to town. That's all the excuse he'd need to fire me."

"So long as you leave Tracey alone, this will go no farther."

"I will. I promise!"

"See that you do, Murphy, or I'll be back."

Muttering to himself, Liam hurried away.

"I hope he meant what he said," I told Wes.

"So do I. I couldn't really get a good read on the guy. I don't know whether he sent Tracey those dead roses yesterday or not, but I wouldn't rule him out. Let's swing by her place and tell her what he said. I'm going to ask her to let me know if she hears from him again, even one more time."

"All right, but I should call her first. She may not be home,"

"Good idea. Knowing Tracey, she's as likely to be at work on a Sunday afternoon as she is to be home."

"She does like her job," I agreed.

I waited until we reached the car to phone Tracey, and I caught her just as she was about to go into a movie with some of her friends from work. After Wes briefed her on our conversation with Liam, he asked her to call him if Liam attempted to contact her again, and she assured him she would.

"Today hasn't exactly turned out the way we hoped," I said.

"No, but we can't change what's happened."

I nodded, thinking again about how precious life is.

"Let's go pick up Bear and take him to the park," Wes suggested. "How about that shady one with the little wading pool for dogs?"

"Okay. He really likes that little park. I tend to forget about it because it's on the other side of town. Maybe we could stop at Foster's and pick up some sandwiches and make it a picnic."

Our trip to Foster's netted us more than sandwiches. After we added potato salad, grapes, chips, cookies, and some fancy decorated dog treats, we picked Bear up and headed to the park, which, surprisingly, turned out to be nearly deserted. We saw a couple walking a large hound. The dog bayed loudly in typical hound speak. When Bear tugged on his leash to go toward him, Wes held him back. Soon, the couple wandered off toward the parking lot, and we had the place all to ourselves. The little dog pond was in an enclosed area so that dogs could be off-leash. Bear splashed enthusiastically in the pond, running back and forth between us and the water until he eventually tired of the game.

Bear shook himself, and water droplets flew in every direction before Wes snapped his leash back on, and we headed for a picnic table under a shady tree. I rubbed Bear with a big fluffy towel I'd brought, but because of his dense undercoat, it was all but impossible to dry him completely. Since he was perfectly content with his damp state, I gave up, and he stretched out on the grass beside us while I spread a plastic tablecloth over the picnic table and unpacked our food.

We'd finished eating, and Bear was happily munching a designer dog treat when a big black pick-up truck pulled into the parking lot. Wes saw it, too, and I could feel his body tensing as I leaned against him and he put his arm around me. I held my breath for a few anxious seconds, until two teenage girls jumped out of the truck. One of the girls carried a pink-and-white cross-body pouch, and I saw a little chihuahua with a jaunty pink cap on his head peeking out from inside.

Breathing a sigh of relief, I said, "Well, I guess those girls don't look too dangerous. When I saw that truck, I nearly had a heart attack."

"It startled me, too," Wes admitted, "but you'd be amazed at how many black pick-up trucks are registered in the county."

"I suppose so. Any word on Michael Stanley, today? I know you don't think he's the one who tried to run us down, but you said you were going to keep tabs on him, just in case."

"That I did. I haven't had a report on him yet today, which probably bodes well, but let me make a quick call."

After a short conversation, punctuated by a lot of "rights" and "uh huhs," Wes told me that Michael had acted like a model citizen all day. He'd left the house with his mother in the morning and driven to another home, where he'd picked up an elderly couple. They'd all attended church and then had lunch together at a popular local restaurant. Afterwards, he'd driven the elderly couple back to their house, returned home with his mother, and spent the afternoon washing and waxing his truck and trailer and checking his mowers and other equipment.

"It does sound as though he's reformed," I said. "I wonder who's tailing him. Hint. Hint. From what you've told me, I know the department wouldn't authorize that much overtime to follow an iffy suspect."

"You're right, Ms. DIY Detective." Wes smiled at me.

"Well, are you going to tell me, or do I have to

torture you to get the information?" I asked, and I began to tickle him, as Bear bounced around us.

Wes laughed and held his hands up. "I give up!" Bear chimed in, barking his approval. "I hired a private detective."

"Really?" My voice betrayed my surprise.

"Yup. You're right about the department, so I've probably been grousing too much. I have nothing solid on Michael, but I did want to find out what he's up to. A friend of mine started his own agency a few years back when he retired from the department. He's the one in charge. Just to be on the safe side, I'm going to keep him on the case for a few more days."

"If Michael didn't come at us with his pick-up, then you're still in danger."

"Try not to worry. I'm still sorting through a few other possibilities—relatives of guys I've busted who have a beef with me."

"In the meantime, please be extra careful."

"I will."

Despite Wes's assurance, I was still worried that he was the target of some unknown assailant's wrath. Based on what he'd learned about Michael's behavior, the parolee didn't seem a likely perpetrator. We'd been fortunate to escape the first time, but I had the uneasy feeling that whoever drove the black pick-up wasn't going to be satisfied with a near miss.

What in the world is going on? I asked myself. First, the crazy truck driver tried to hit us; then Tracey received the dead black roses; and today we'd discovered Patty drowning. My neighbor Fran, who's a bit superstitious, would surely say that bad things come in threes. If only that were true, then perhaps the bad karma had ended, but I didn't really believe it myself.

Unfortunately, the next morning, I awoke to more

bad news. Bear woke up early, as usual, and I could hear rain pounding the roof. It was coming down hard, and when I tried to let Bear out, he balked and wouldn't venture outside. So I fed him his breakfast and sat down with a cup of coffee to watch the early morning news.

That's when I heard that Patty had died without ever recovering consciousness. Her death was reported as a drowning accident, followed by an interview with a safety expert who'd put together a list of tips to prevent accidental drownings. Evidently, the police hadn't publicized the fact that Patty's drowning was suspicious. I thought about poor Megan. Although I knew Tara would do her best to comfort Megan, at such terrible times, relatives were often the ones a bereaved person turned to. I hoped that Lisa would step up and offer her niece some much-needed support although she certainly hadn't shown much concern for either her sister or her niece yesterday.

By mid-morning, the rain had stopped, and Bear was splashing about in the little puddles of water that had pooled on the patio. I'd already answered loads of phone calls from friends and neighbors in Hawkeye Haven, all expressing surprise at the news of Patty's drowning. The universal sentiment I heard from them was that, although they had disliked the woman because she'd caused so much havoc during her reign of terror as Hawkeye Haven's manager, they believed that the accidental death of someone so young was tragic. I realized that, at 36, Patty was only a couple years younger than I, and it was a sobering thought.

I didn't have Megan's phone number, so I called Tara to find out if there was anything I could do for Megan. I wasn't able to get through, and I couldn't even leave a voice mail, because her mailbox was full, so I texted Tara. There wasn't much else I could do except wait for her response.

Shooing Bear into the yard, I took a wide push broom and swept the water off the patio. Now that the sun had come out, the humidity combined with the heat was going to make for a very sticky day, but it also meant that the air conditioning would be cranked up to the max at Alberto's, where I was meeting Amy, Cynthia, and Jennifer for lunch at noon.

After a quick survey of my closet, I decided to wear a teal cotton double-gauze maxi dress with loose, long sleeves. It would probably feel too hot when I was outside in the sun and too cool when I was in the restaurant, but, at least, I wouldn't have to drag along a jacket or sweater. I took my time getting ready, putting on some eye make-up with a light touch and lingering over my jewelry collection before deciding on which earrings and necklace to wear. My bruises, now a shade of purple, looked as ugly as ever, but my maxi dress hid my legs, and usually nobody noticed my bruised palms. There was little use trying to hide them anyway. I certainly wasn't going to wear gloves in the summer, with the exception of the wedding. I'd decided it would be a good idea to wear the fingerless lace gloves on the Big Day, so there'd be nary a hint of the run-for-our-lives incident Wes and I had experienced.

As I left the house, I told Bear to be a good boy. He stared at me forlornly in his usual attempt to guilt trip me. He always managed to make me feel sorry for leaving him at home, despite the fact that I knew for sure that he napped most of the time I was gone.

When I arrived at the community center, my stomach churned when I saw a black pick-up truck coming toward me. It was pulling a trailer.

"Stanley Lawn Service" was emblazoned on its side.

Chapter 9

I told myself there was nothing to worry about. After all, the pick-up was leaving. I snagged a parking space right in front and joined Luke, who was standing on the sidewalk, watching the landscaper depart.

"Hi, Luke," I said. "Do you know who was in that black pick-up that just pulled out?"

Luke nodded. "Some guy who wanted to ask about doing landscape work for Hawkeye Haven, but, of course, we already have a company contracted. Anyway, one guy couldn't possibly handle Hawkeye Haven's account. He'd need a big crew and lots more equipment than one pick-up truck and trailer. I'd say he's trying to bite off more than he can chew, in this case. I guess I shouldn't have laughed at him when he asked about it, though. He looked awfully dejected when I told him the score."

"Dejected, rather than angry?"

"Yeah, definitely. He gave me some of his cards and said that if I or anyone I know needed some yard work done to give him a call. He even said 'please'!"

Evidently, Michael was busy trying to hustle up some more work. His visit to Hawkeye Haven seemed innocent enough, but I called Wes, anyway, to let him know that I'd seen Michael. He didn't answer, which was often the case when he was at work, so, as I headed next door to Alberto's, I texted him to let him know that Michael had visited Hawkeye Haven to look for work.

The host greeted me and asked if I had a reservation.

He was the same host who'd been on duty the night Liz and the colonel had met at a raucous meeting of Hawkeye Haven's HOA. After the meeting, the three of us had come over to Alberto's to commiserate over dessert about the high-handed tactics of the HOA and its manager, Patty. The colonel had raised an eyebrow when he'd seen the host's diamond stud earring, shoulder-length hair, and tattooed forearms, but he'd refrained from commenting on them.

I saw Jennifer sitting at a table in the far corner. She noticed me at about the same time and waved as the host led me to the table. There was a woman, her back to me, sitting with Jennifer, but it wasn't Amy or Cynthia. Perhaps Jennifer had invited someone else to join us. After all, we probably wouldn't be seeing Jennifer again soon since she was going to Chicago at the end of the week. Once her house was sold, she'd make the move to Chicago permanent, and we might never see her again.

A few steps ahead of me, the host pulled out the chair on Jennifer's left and waited to seat me. As I came closer, I could see that Lisa was the woman who'd had her back to me. I greeted Jennifer, who shook hands with Lisa before almost immediately excusing herself to make a business call, and I was left sitting alone with Lisa.

"I'm sorry for your loss, Lisa," I said. "I heard about Patty's death on the news this morning."

Lisa shrugged. "Life goes on. I always told her those silly shoes would be the death of her. And guess what? They were. I'll never understand why she insisted on wearing six-inch heels to work."

Obviously, the police hadn't yet informed Lisa that her sister's death was no accident. That fact hadn't been reported on television, either. Since it wasn't public knowledge, I realized I shouldn't be the one to tell Lisa that her sister had been murdered.

"How's Megan coping?"

"About like you'd expect—not well. I couldn't take listening to her moaning and crying any longer, and I have a full schedule of appointments today, so I dropped her off at her friend's house."

Quite the caring aunt, I thought. Poor Megan. Lisa didn't want to be near her because she was understandably upset by her mother's death. Strangely, Lisa didn't seem upset at all. I would have been more surprised by her attitude if I hadn't been at the hospital yesterday where she'd been more concerned with business than her sister's "accident" and hadn't even bothered to see Patty in the emergency room. By this point, I was pretty much at a loss for words, but I didn't need to worry. Lisa continued the conversation herself.

"By the way, Laurel, I want to thank you for recommending me to your friend Jennifer. I've just listed her house." She picked up some documents from the tabletop and slipped them into her black leather portfolio. "I was on the verge of cutting you and Wes loose because you two can't seem to make up your minds, but considering that you threw some business my way, I'll keep you on for a while. But don't forget. I can't go on like this indefinitely. You need to make a decision and put in an offer."

I was so stunned by this pronouncement that I was literally speechless.

"Call me," she directed and walked briskly away, leaving me gaping at her back.

I'd barely recovered myself when Jennifer returned to the table with an apology for leaving to make her phone call.

"It's just that there's so much to do to launch my

design business that I'm starting to feel overwhelmed. Dealing with business—well, it's all new to me. Matt never discussed business with me, and he handled all our finances, so it's taking me a while to get up to speed."

"I understand," I assured her. "Lisa said that you decided to list your house with her."

"Yes. I showed her the place yesterday afternoon, and I also spoke with a broker from another real estate agency yesterday evening. Lisa had a far better sales record than the other agent I interviewed, and she's sold several properties here in Hawkeye Haven, so she's familiar with the community. She seemed like the best choice, especially since she's working with several buyers who are looking for a big house in Hawkeye Haven. She's already lined up two showings for this afternoon."

"Fast work," I commented with a frown.

"Is something wrong, Laurel?"

"It's just that I find her attitude baffling. I'm sure she's good at sales; her numbers don't lie, but I can't understand why she doesn't seem upset at all by her sister's death."

"Did her sister die recently or has it been a while?"

"Last night. Actually, Wes and I discovered Patty floating in the pool when we went to look at a house yesterday. She wasn't breathing, but Wes did CPR, and she was hanging on when the paramedics took her to the hospital. According to the news report I heard this morning, she never did regain consciousness, though."

"That's terrible. Lisa never said a word about it."

Jennifer looked past me, and I turned to see Amy and Cynthia coming in. We waved, and they spotted us before the host approached them. After we ordered our meals, Jennifer pressed me to repeat my story to Amy and Cynthia. Although neither of them knew Lisa, they knew Patty, remembering how happy the residents of Hawkeye Haven had been when Patty's contract with the HOA had been canceled.

"It's awful the way she died," Cynthia said. "Unfortunately, I don't think anyone in Hawkeye Haven will miss her. She was a dishonest schemer, and she actually seemed to enjoy making life miserable for the residents."

"I know one person who'll miss her," I said, "and that's her daughter Megan. She came to one of my classes, and she's quite a timid young woman. When she found out what happened to Patty, she was devastated. On top of that, she's not getting any support from her aunt—that's Patty's sister Lisa, the real estate agent Wes and I have been working with."

"And the same agent I just listed my house with," Jennifer chimed in.

"At least, Megan has one good friend who's giving her lots of support," I said. "Tara Nichols came to the hospital to be with Megan yesterday, and Lisa told me herself that she took Megan to Tara's house on her way to work this morning."

"Oh, I know Tara," Amy said. "She's such a darling, a very caring person. She always senses when someone needs a hand and does anything she can to help, so I know she'll do her best to console Megan."

"That's a fact," Cynthia said. "Tara does a lot of work placing stray pets, too. I know she's adopted a couple homeless cats and a dog herself. Ironically, last year Patty fined her several times for having more pets than the HOA allows, but Colette looks the other way unless the pets are bothering the neighbors. That's never the case with Tara's pets, though."

I hadn't known Tara until she signed up to take my

DIY Bridal Crafts class, and I still didn't know her very well, but Amy and Cynthia had just confirmed my favorable impression of her. Although Lisa's attitude puzzled me, I felt a bit better, because Tara would be there for Megan.

I tried not to look too envious as Jennifer, Amy, and Cynthia munched on Alberto's signature bruschetta as we waited for the meals we'd ordered.

When our server arrived with our lunches, I looked covetously at my companions' plates. I had ordered a tomato-and-cucumber salad, and it looked puny next to my friends' lunches.

"Laurel, would you like some of this super cheesy grilled sandwich?" Amy asked. "With all these fries and salad on the side, I have more than plenty."

"No, thanks, Amy," I replied. "I would like it, of course, but I'm determined to diet the rest of the week. I've had too many big meals and desserts lately, and they've all been delicious, but I want to make absolutely sure my wedding gown will fit just right."

"You don't look as though you've gained any weight," Jennifer commented. "Not like me."

Jennifer had gained about ten or fifteen pounds since her husband's death, but she'd been painfully thin before, so it looked good on her.

"Jennifer, you look fabulous," Cynthia reassured her. "And so does Laurel. I could certainly lose a few pounds—well, more than a few, I guess, but I just like to eat too much, so I don't feel very motivated. I've tried all kinds of diets, but it's always such a struggle that I give up on them after a week or two. I think you have the right idea, Amy. You exercise so much that you burn tons of calories."

"I guess I'm lucky," Amy said. "I don't exercise to maintain my weight, but it's a great side benefit."

Petite Amy, who stood just five feet high, ate whatever she wanted, seldom skipped dessert, and never gained an ounce. She was the envy of all our friends and neighbors. Few of us would want to match her pace in exercise, though. She swam, golfed, and played tennis, but her daily practices for competition ballroom dancing undoubtedly expended the most calories.

"How's the new dance routine coming along?" I asked.

"Not bad. Bud choreographed both our new routines himself. They're both more challenging than the ones we danced in the last competition, but I think we'll do all right."

"I *know* you'll do more than all right," I said. "Last time you won the tango and cha-cha competitions."

"But we took second place in foxtrot, so, this time, we really want to try for first prize. That's why we're skipping the cha-cha and concentrating just on the tango and the foxtrot, especially the foxtrot. Down the road, we're planning on expanding our repertoire, but, for now, we're sticking to just two dances."

"That's fantastic, Amy," Jennifer said. "I've always thought of exercise as a kind of necessary evil that I forced myself to do, but it's fun for you, instead of drudgery."

"It *is* fun," Amy agreed. "I like other sports, but I'm really glad that I'm back into dancing. If I hadn't unexpectedly discovered that Bud could dance that night a few months back at the FFF fundraiser, I probably never would have gone back to it."

"Speaking of FFF," Cynthia interjected, "there's something I need to tell you all." Cynthia lowered her voice to a level that the other diners sitting nearby wouldn't be able to hear. We all leaned forward slightly to catch what she said. "Remember when we were at the shower Saturday and I said I'd seen Marcie at the grocery store?" We all nodded. "Well, I've seen her again, this time up close and personal. I went into the office early this morning, just like I usually do. I can get a lot accomplished when nobody else is around. And there she was, bold as brass, waiting for me in my office!"

"You're kidding!" Amy exclaimed. "How did she get in? We had all the locks changed after the board fired her."

"After she left, I found out that one of the building's maintenance workers let her in. He recognized her, and he didn't realize she no longer worked at FFF, so when she told him she'd forgotten her keys, he unlocked the door for her with the master key. By the way, I made sure that won't ever happen again."

"I can't believe she had the nerve to come back to Center City," I said, "let alone come to FFF's offices. What did she want?"

"Well, you're not going to believe this, either," Cynthia said, "but she wants her old job back; she wants to take over as director of FFF again."

"That's crazy!" Jennifer said. "After she embezzled money from a *charity* and refused to take any responsibility for her actions, she wants to come back? Unbelievable!"

"I was so flabbergasted at her appearance I was at a loss for words. You all know me, and that doesn't happen very often. Marcie said I was no better than a caretaker and that, as its founder, she knew more about FFF and how to raise money than anybody else. She passed off her embezzlement as just a bonus that she rightly deserved because her salary was too low, and she said that it shouldn't have made a blip on the board's radar. I reminded her that there was a warrant out for her arrest, and her bravado sagged a little then.

"She insisted that I call an emergency board meeting so that she could negotiate terms with the board and have the charges against her dismissed. I told her that the board couldn't dismiss the charges, even if they wanted to. Only the district attorney could do that. She seemed convinced that he'd drop the charges on the board's request."

"I doubt that," I said, "but, from what I've heard about him from Wes, he might possibly be open to a plea deal. The problem is that Marcie has no remorse whatsoever for what she's done. She doesn't think it was wrong. I just can't see the DA dismissing charges against her when she has that attitude."

"Neither can I. I don't think that we'd have anything to gain by meeting with her. Last time we met with her, she refused to listen to us, and she left right in the middle of the meeting," Amy said.

"Slamming the door on her way out," I added.

"What do you think we should do?" Cynthia asked. "I reminded her that I don't have the authority to call an emergency board meeting, in any case."

"Right. FFF's by-laws specify that it takes two board members to call one, and we have to give twenty-four hours' notice," I said, thinking back to a few months ago when we'd had to call an emergency board meeting because an audit of FFF's finances I had initiated had uncovered Marcie's embezzlement. "Amy, you're the board president now. What do you think?"

"Ugh. I don't know whether we should do it or not," Amy replied. "I don't look forward to seeing Marcie again, especially after the way she stormed out of the last meeting. It doesn't sound as though she plans to offer to repay any of the money she stole."

"I still haven't forgiven her for not showing up to speak at Matt's funeral," Jennifer said. "I guess that's a small thing compared to her embezzlement, but here's a woman who was in our book club for several months, so she's been a guest in all our homes, and this is how she acts. I think we ought to call the police and let them know she's back in town, maybe even hire a private investigator to find out where she's staying. If we could locate her, they could pick her up, and the district attorney could prosecute her."

"She wouldn't have the nerve to stay at her own house, would she?" Amy asked.

"From the way she acted this morning at the office, I'd guess she's bold enough to stay there, but, as it turns out, she doesn't own the property herself," Cynthia said. "Her neighbor, Viola Bennett, owns it and was leasing it to Marcie. Viola substitutes once in a while in our golf foursome, when one of us can't play. Viola mentioned that she'd rented the house to Marcie several months ago, so I really didn't give it much thought at the time. Marcie was cagey about how to contact her if we decided to have an emergency board meeting, as she suggested. She wouldn't give me her cell phone number, but said she'd call me back. She's erased all her social media profiles, so there aren't any clues there, either."

"I suppose we could call the emergency meeting for tomorrow afternoon, since Amy and I are both on the board," I said. "Then we could try to convince her to set up a payment plan to make restitution to FFF for the money she embezzled. If she doesn't go for that, we could call the police and ask them to serve the warrant."

"Maybe we should call a meeting. It's not fair for us to make any decisions without the other board members," Amy said.

We all agreed that the other board members should be aware of the situation and that Amy and I should give the required twenty-four-hour notice to the other board members. Although Cynthia, as acting director of FFF, attended board meetings, she wasn't a voting member. Jennifer's late husband had been a board member, bequeathing a huge sum to the organization in his will, and Jennifer had been instrumental in making sure that his donation was disbursed, despite Marcie's embezzlement. Since then, she'd contributed a substantial amount of money herself to FFF.

Dessert menus in hand, our server approached the table, and we leaned back in our chairs. Cynthia and Amy accepted the little dessert menus while Jennifer and I declined. My tomato-and-cucumber salad hadn't been especially filling, and I would have loved to indulge in one of Alberto's decadent brownie sundaes, but I refrained. Wes and I were due at Liz's for dinner at six-thirty, and there'd be more food there to tempt me. I kept silently reminding myself that it would be worth it to maintain my resolve when my wedding gown fit perfectly on my wedding day.

When the desserts arrived, I was glad I had ordered a cup of coffee to sip. Since I preferred my coffee black, skipping cream and sugar wouldn't present a hardship, and I wouldn't be adding any unwanted calories to my diet. As Amy picked up her fork, I stared enviously at the lemon meringue pie she'd ordered. Its lightly browned meringue was piled high, fluffy and inviting, with graceful swirls on the top. Cynthia's carrot cake looked just as good, its thick cream cheese frosting providing a nice contrast to the miniature orange carrot with green leaves Alberto's pastry chef had expertly piped on its top. I didn't usually obsess over food, but I was beginning to understand why Cynthia found it so difficult to diet. I'd been dieting less than a day, and I already felt hungry.

After lunch, Amy and I remained at the table for a few minutes. We each texted half the board members to let them know about the emergency meeting, which we set for three o'clock the next afternoon. By the time we left, we'd received confirmations from most of the board that they'd be attending. We only needed a majority for a quorum, so it looked as though the meeting would be a go. I wasn't looking forward to it in the slightest. In fact, I'd deliberately arranged my schedule ahead of time so that I'd have a pleasant and calm few days before the wedding. So far, it certainly wasn't turning out the way I'd planned, but there was no predicting unforeseen circumstances.

I knew Amy felt just as dubious about the upcoming meeting as I did.

"See you tomorrow," she said glumly, as we left the restaurant together. As president of FFF, Amy would likely be the first target of Marcie's wrath, if tomorrow's meeting was anything like the meeting when we'd confronted her about her embezzlement. I tried to put the whole sorry mess out of my mind as I drove home, and when Bear greeted me joyfully as I came in, I succeeded in forgetting it for a while.

After I gave him a hug, Bear ran to the patio door, whipping his head back and forth in an effort to convince me to play fetch with him. Despite the sticky heat, I went outside with him. At first, neither of us saw his hard rubber ball, but eventually he found it under a dense, leafy bush, retrieved it, and, dropping it at my feet, looked up at me expectantly. I played with him longer than I'd intended, and, by the time we went back inside to the air-conditioned comfort of the house, I was drenched in perspiration. I headed for the shower while

Bear flopped down on the cool tile in the kitchen, in hopes of begging for a snack when I finished. After I showered, his hopes were rewarded when I fed him several baby carrots, which he consumed with relish. As always, he begged for more, but when I said "all gone," he got the message and lay down again while I popped the damp clothing I'd worn earlier into the washing machine, set it on the gentle cycle, and turned on the machine.

I couldn't help thinking about Patty and wondering who had attacked her. As Cynthia had said, she'd been extremely unpopular with the homeowners of Hawkeye Haven. Her harassment of residents and her efforts to assess undeserved fines had earned her plenty of enemies, but she'd been fired many months ago, and I thought the residents pretty much considered her firing as the removal of a thorn from their sides. From what I'd heard, Colette had been instrumental in resolving the problems Patty had caused. She'd waived bogus fines and cancelled collection actions that Patty had initiated. By now, grateful residents had all but forgotten about Patty and her underhanded ways.

Patty surely had other enemies, though, or one, at least. Since Lisa evidently hadn't asked Patty to substitute for her until the last moment, I doubted that many other people knew about it, besides maybe the receptionist at the office of Gold Medal Real Estate. Lisa hadn't even bothered to let Wes or me know that Patty, instead of Lisa herself, would be showing us the house at 2132 Maquoketa. Still, I supposed that someone could have followed Patty, looking for an opportunity to catch her alone and do her harm.

What kept nagging me was Lisa's uncaring attitude about her own sister's death. I could understand that she might be driven to succeed in her career, but at the expense of everything else in her life? She'd exhibited a callous disregard for her niece's feelings, which also confused me because, according to what my student Heather had told me at our final DIY Bridal Crafts class, Megan had practically been raised by her aunt, yet Lisa seemed far more concerned with her next real estate deal than she did with poor Megan.

Wes always said the police looked to the family first in a homicide investigation. Lisa was definitely the one person who knew for sure exactly where Patty would be when she was attacked. Could Lisa have killed her own sister?

Chapter 10

Since I didn't know enough about the two sisters' relationship to be able to think of a credible motive, I didn't dwell on the thought. Surely by now, Walker or Smith must have caught up to Lisa long enough to interview her.

Wes called, and I didn't need to remind him that we were due at Liz's for a barbeque at six-thirty. Since it was informal, he said he'd go home to change from his suit into casual clothes before he came over. He let me know that he was still having Michael followed, and, so far, his friend, the retired cop turned private investigator, hadn't uncovered anything suspicious. Wes's mention of the private investigator gave me an idea, but, since I knew Wes had to get back to work, I decided to broach it with him later in the evening.

Wes had just rung off when Tara called, apologizing for taking so long to get back to me.

"That's okay, Tara," I said. "I wanted to check on Megan. After I texted you, I happened to run into Lisa at Alberto's, and she told me that she'd dropped Megan off at your house. I couldn't believe that she wouldn't stay with Megan the day her mother died, but all she seems to care about is her real estate business."

"That's a fact," Tara agreed. "Megan's resting upstairs right now, so I took the opportunity to return all my calls and texts that have been piling up. To answer your question, she's in a bad way. She's cried so much that she's exhausted herself, and I finally convinced her to lie down for a while. Even if she's not able to go to sleep, she may be able to rest for an hour or so. Honestly, Laurel, that aunt of hers has to be the most uncaring person I've ever heard of. She literally dumped Megan off here early this morning and left before I opened the front door. Of course, I'm happy to have Megan here and help her in any way I can, but I didn't know she was coming! What if I hadn't been home? Poor Megan would have been left on my doorstep all alone, and at a time like this! I've never actually met Lisa, but when I do, I'm going to give her a piece of my mind. That's for sure!"

"That's awful," I said. "I'm a bit confused. I can't understand why Lisa's acting the way she is when she was the one who looked after Megan when she was growing up, or did I get that wrong?"

"No, I did," Tara said. "When Megan told me her aunt brought her up, I assumed it was the same aunt she was staying with here, but I was mistaken. Megan's aunt Erica brought her up, but she's overseas right now. Megan told me she's an interpreter for a big company that just opened a branch in Switzerland. When Megan decided to come here for the summer, she'd planned to stay with her mother, but Patty had a fire in her apartment a few days before Megan arrived, so they were both staying at Lisa's house."

"Well, I'm glad to know that Megan has other family because she can't depend on Lisa. You've been a good friend to Megan, and she certainly needs one very badly now. Is there anything I can do to help?"

"Yes, there is, but I hate to ask you because I know you're busy with your wedding preparations."

"We're trying to keep the wedding small and simple, and everything's pretty much as ready as it can be, actually. So tell me: what can I do to help?"

"Can you drive Megan to Des Moines tomorrow morning to meet her grandparents at the airport? I'd be happy to do it myself, but I volunteer at the animal shelter every Tuesday, and they're so short on helpers; I hate to miss a day."

"Of course, I can. Fill me in on the details, and I'll pick Megan up in the morning."

"Okay, thanks, Laurel. I really appreciate it. Megan's grandparents will be arriving on a flight from Los Angeles, but they can't rent a car because neither one of them is able to drive anymore. She said her grandmother's using a wheelchair, and her grandfather can't move his left arm, due to a stroke, so Megan wants to meet them right in the baggage claim area. It's hard to believe that their own daughter wouldn't meet them. Lisa had the nerve to suggest that they take the shuttle from the airport to Center City."

"That's crazy! Don't worry. I'm happy to help. Just let me know where and when to pick Megan up, and I'll be there."

"Great! Let me double check the flight schedule with Megan later, and I'll call or text you the details."

Pleased that I could do something for Megan but more disgusted than ever at Lisa's disregard for her own niece, I said good-bye to Tara.

Since Liz had insisted that we bring Bear with us to swim in her pool, I decided to feed him his dinner a bit earlier than usual. I didn't like for him to do heavy exercise right after eating. Like most Labs, Bear loved the water, and he loved swimming. I was a little apprehensive about bringing him to a barbeque, though, because he loved eating just as much as swimming, and he'd surely beg for some snacks, but I resolved to keep them to a minimum and insist that he lie down while the four of us had dinner outside on the patio. Liz didn't normally barbeque, but the colonel fancied himself something of a barbeque wizard. He had invented his own secret recipe for barbeque sauce, and he'd won a couple of prizes at local barbeque competitions. If I hadn't promised myself I'd stick to my diet, I might have been eager to do more than just sample the colonel's cooking, especially since my stomach had been rumbling for the last hour. As it was, I'd already let Liz know that I'd be strictly limiting my calorie count, and she understood. She assured me that grilled chicken and vegetables were great diet foods, so I'd be able to eat while keeping my calorie count low for the day.

I dressed in tan cotton slacks, a loose, green, lightweight top, and tan sandals. Then I added a long chain necklace with a tassel and some tassel earrings I'd made out of a delicate chain. Liz always sported perfect make-up. I decided to change my own usual low maintenance make-up routine so that I wouldn't look pale beside her. I carefully applied eye liner, mascara, and a bit of pale green eye shadow. I swiped some lip-color gloss on, and called it a day. My skill in applying make-up would never match Liz's, but I was satisfied with my results.

"Wow! Hi, gorgeous," Wes greeted me when he came to the door. We hugged before Bear jumped between us, looking for attention from his buddy.

As Bear flopped over for a tummy rub, Wes said, "He's going with us, isn't he?"

"Yes. He doesn't get left behind this evening. I'll grab his leash."

When I returned with the leash and a big, fluffy towel, Bear pranced around me, panting in excitement. "Hold still, Bear," He cooperated long enough for me to snap the leash on his collar. We went through the side yard to the gate to Liz's backyard, which she'd unlocked in anticipation of our arrival. Liz and the colonel greeted us. As soon as Bear spied the colonel, he sat down in front of him and proffered his paw, which the colonel shook politely. After that, Bear moved to Liz who petted him, much to the disgust of her cat Miss Muffett, who was watching us from the other side of the glass patio door. Miss Muffett wasn't allowed outside, and we were careful to keep cat and dog separated since Bear liked to chase cats, and we'd learned to our dismay, that Miss Muffett was no exception.

Having greeted his hosts, Bear turned to me and whined softly. I freed him of his collar and leash, and he wasted no time in plunging into the pool and paddling around in circles. Every so often, he'd climb the steps at the shallow end of the pool, emerge, run around the yard, and then head back to the pool.

The scent of grilling chicken wafted our way as the colonel tended to the barbeque, while he and Wes talked, and Liz and I set the table on the patio for four. Liz brought out a bowl of water for Bear and set it next to the pool while Bear continued to swim.

My stomach was rumbling so much now that I felt conspicuous, but neither Wes nor the colonel noticed, and Liz didn't say anything. By the time the colonel had basted the chicken in his special barbeque sauce and transferred baked potatoes and vegetables wrapped in foil to serving platters, I was feeling as though I could eat my weight in food, but I restrained myself and ate only a half chicken breast, grilled asparagus, and some salad. Feeling deprived, I turned down Liz's offer of a glass of wine and, instead, drank iced tea without any sugar. I splurged just the least little bit by adding an extra tablespoonful of barbeque sauce to my grilled chicken, but I figured I was still under the thousand calorie mark I'd set as my target for the day.

Bear was so busy splashing in the pool that, for once, he didn't come over and beg for a snack. A breeze was carrying the aroma of food away from him, so perhaps that was a factor.

"Doesn't he ever get tired?" Liz asked as she served the colonel and Wes strawberry shortcake topped with real whipped cream while Liz and I each settled for a small bowl of strawberries, no sugar added.

"He really loves to swim," I said, watching as Bear paddled around the pool for the umteenth time,"but I predict he's going to give up soon."

After we finished dessert, Liz and I quickly cleared the table. I popped the dishes into the dishwasher while Liz put away the leftovers. She offered me a glass of wine, but I opted for another glass of iced tea. We grabbed a couple bottles of beer for the men and joined them on the patio, taking care not to let Miss Muffett, who was lurking near the door, outside.

Liz had recently purchased new wicker patio furniture with comfy, plush cushions. Wes and I sat on the loveseat, while the colonel settled himself in a rocker and Liz sat next to him in a side chair. The light breeze kept the warm air moving as the sun dropped lower in the sky, and the clouds turned a vibrant shade of pink. Wes reached for my hand and held it while we all chatted and watched Bear slowly circle the pool once more. It was a perfect summer's evening.

Bear finally got out of the pool, taking a bit longer to climb the steps this time. He took a few steps away from the pool, out onto the grassy lawn, and shook himself mightily. He was far enough away from us that we didn't get sprayed by the droplets of pool water that he was shedding.

"Good job, Bear," I said, as I jumped up, reached for his towel, and slung it over his back. I rubbed his fur vigorously, until the towel was wet, before releasing him. I asked Wes to drape the towel over the wall that separated Liz's backyard from mine since he was a few inches taller than the wall, and it was a much easier reach for him than it was for me. I'd let it dry there overnight and snag it from my own backyard for the laundry in the morning.

Wagging his tail, Bear followed Wes and me back to the loveseat and plopped down in front of us, his head on top of my foot, and soon fell asleep. Bear softly snored, and we talked quietly, as dusk descended. Just as I was thinking that the peaceful evening was the remedy I needed to forget, as least for a short while, the chaos of the last few days, Bear's ears perked up as he jerked awake. Alert now, he lifted his head and then sat up.

"He must have heard something," the colonel observed.

"He has better ears than I do," Liz replied. "I didn't hear a thing."

Suddenly, Bear jumped up and ran to the gate, where he began to bark loudly.

"Maybe I'd better take a look," Wes said as he got up and went to the gate. "What is it, boy?"

Bear was barking louder now and sounded quite ferocious.

"I think I'll take a look around," Wes said. "You don't happen to have a flashlight handy, do you, Liz?"

"Right in the kitchen," she said. "Top drawer on the left."

"I'll get it," the colonel offered. "You girls stay here, and we'll take a look around. It's probably nothing to worry about. Could even be a raccoon. We've had some sightings over near the golf course lately."

I quickly snapped Bear's collar and leash back on and held him back as Wes and the colonel went out the gate. "Come on, Bear. Stay here with mommy," I said as I coaxed him back toward the patio. He'd stopped barking and no longer seemed perturbed, and I would have agreed with the colonel's assessment that there was nothing to worry about if it hadn't been for the growl that had preceded Bear's barking and the urgency I'd sensed in it.

It sounded exactly like the way he'd barked when the strange delivery man had come to Tracey's door bearing dead, black roses.

Chapter 11

When Wes and the colonel returned, they reported that they hadn't found anybody snooping around the neighborhood. In fact, they hadn't seen anybody outside at all. They had watched a furry animal scurrying down the street toward the golf course, and the colonel concluded that it had been one of the raccoons that the course maintenance workers had noticed several times in the past week.

Bear certainly paid attention whenever he saw a rabbit or a cat he wanted to chase, so I supposed a raccoon would interest him, too. Maybe I was imagining that his bark had sounded different and his growl menacing. After all, he'd awakened from a deep sleep just before he started to bark, and he'd calmed down rapidly.

Wes relaxed as he joined me once again on the loveseat and Bear lay back down to snooze while Liz and I decided that now would be a good time to make a list of the flower arrangements we'd need for the wedding Saturday.

"Let's start with the bride," Liz said, her pen poised above her notebook. "Your bouquet's the most important arrangement, so we want it to be absolutely lovely. Fran has some nice, large white roses coming on that should be just right in a few days. My white daisies are looking good, and I also have some lavender and yellow daisies, but it seems to me that the roses would go better with your glamorous gown."

"I think so, too. The roses sound perfect."

"Okay. We'll go with the roses for the bride." Liz beamed, jotting down some notes. "Laurel's going to be such a beautiful bride, don't you agree, Wes?"

When Wes didn't answer, we turned to him and saw that he was fast asleep. Liz put her finger to her lips and spoke more softly.

"No need to wake him yet," she said. "Along with the roses, I think some Queen Anne's lace would look nice in your bouquet. I'd like to wrap the base of your bouquet in a pretty white lace handkerchief I've had since the fifties. It can be your 'something borrowed.'"

"Fabulous!" I whispered.

"Remind me again what color Tracey's dress is."

"She's going to wear a short sheath dress with kind of an abstract design in cool pastels—mint green, baby blue, and lavender."

"You didn't happen to make it from that jersey fabric you were dying out in the backyard last month, did you?"

"The very same. That gives me an idea. I still have some of that fabric. What if I hem a square of it, and you can wrap the base of her bouquet in it so that it'll match her dress."

"Great. How about a combination of yellow daisies, white roses, and lavender daisies for her bouquet?"

"Sounds good to me," I said, and Liz made another notation in her notebook.

"To coordinate, we can make the boutonnières and corsages from white roses, too, and if you have enough fabric scraps left, we can make bias strips to use for bows, instead of ribbon. Now, let's see. How many corsages will we need?"

"I think just two, one for my mom and one for Wes's mom. No. Wait. I can't leave out Aunt Ellen—she's

Tracey's mom. She'll need one, too, so three in all. We'd better add another one for Wes's sister Denise."

"Right," Liz said, scribbling in her notebook. "And for the men? Four as well?"

"Yes. Dad, Wes's dad, Uncle Bill, and Jack, Wes's brother-in-law, should all have a boutonnière, even though Uncle Bill probably won't want to wear his, but I'll bet Aunt Ellen will make him do it. He thinks he's too macho to wear a flower."

"Oh, pooh! I'm sure he can stand it for a few hours."

"I'm sure he can," I agreed, smiling. "Like I said, Aunt Ellen will see to it."

Soft snoring interrupted us, but Wes wasn't the culprit. The colonel had fallen asleep, too. At my feet, Bear's legs were moving as though he were running. He was dreaming, probably of chasing a rabbit or maybe Miss Muffett.

"Liz, I think it's time for us to get going. Evidently, we're boring the men to sleep."

We laughed as I gently shook Wes and patted Bear. Liz nudged the colonel who awoke with a start.

"Sorry," Wes and the colonel said in unison, looking sheepish.

"And we're sorry we were boring you boys," Liz claimed, with a wink.

Of course, they both protested that wasn't the case.

After thanking Liz and the colonel for their hospitality, we left by the side gate. Once again, Bear started barking, but this time it sounded like his friendly, excited bark. We looked toward the front sidewalk where my neighbors Fran, Brian, and their golden retriever Goldie were visible in the glow of the street light. They stopped when they heard Bear, and we joined them.

Bear and Goldie wagged their tails and nuzzled each

other companionably. Fran and Brian often did dogsitting duty for me when I'd be gone for several hours, and I returned the favor by looking after Goldie for them whenever the need arose. Since Bear and Goldie got along so well, we all thought we had a good thing going.

"Goldie's going to be thrilled to have Bear to play with next week," Fran said.

"I can't thank you enough for taking care of Bear while we're on our honeymoon," I said. My parents would be staying at my house with Bear for a couple days after the wedding, but they were planning to return to Seattle on Tuesday with Aunt Ellen and Uncle Bill. Since Tracey had been able to get only one day off on Monday, and she worked such long hours, they knew they wouldn't be able to see much of her when she was working. When my parents left, Bear would be going to stay with Fran and Brian until we returned from our honeymoon. Although Bear would be in good hands the whole time we were gone, I knew I'd miss him, but I also knew I was very fortunate that he'd have such good care while Wes and I were gone. Bear would be happy at home with my parents, and he'd be happy to stay with Fran, Brian, and Goldie.

"I know Bear will love it," I replied. "I hate to ask you another favor, but do you think you could watch Bear tomorrow, too? I'll be gone most of the morning, and I have an afternoon meeting I have to attend. There may be time to come home in the early afternoon, but maybe not." I explained that I'd be picking up Megan's grandparents from the airport in Des Moines, but if the flight happened to be late, I could be delayed.

"Sure. That's no problem," Brian said. "We were planning on taking Goldie to the park tomorrow morning, so Bear can come along. They'll be tired after that, and they'll probably sleep most of the afternoon. I might do the same. Old age is catching up with me, you know."

"Oh, silly," Fran said, nudging her husband. "You're only sixty-three."

He grinned. "Well, I might not be as decrepit as I let on sometimes, but I'll tell you one thing: retirement has made me lazy, and, if I feel like taking a nap in the middle of the afternoon, I take one. When I was working, I thought nothing of putting in a fourteen-or fifteen-hour work day."

"I can relate to that," Wes said. "I've put in quite a few of those long days myself, but the boss is going easy on me this week; he promised to give any new cases to other detectives."

Just then Wes's cell phone rang. He glanced at the display and immediately picked up. From the one-sided conversation, I could tell that he'd been called in to work.

"Well, that didn't last long," he said. "Sorry, I have to go." He turned to me. "Let me at least walk you to your door."

"It's okay, Wes," I said, giving him a quick kiss. "We're practically on the doorstep now. I'll be fine."

"We'll make sure of it," Brian promised.

"I'll call you, sweetheart." After a hug for me and a pat for Bear, Wes pulled his car keys out of his pocket and left, waving as he drove away.

"Poor guy," Brian said. "No rest for the weary, I guess."

"Wes does work a lot of overtime," I said, "but he's so used to it, I think he copes pretty well. I guess I've gotten used to it, too."

"That's good," Fran said, "because I think you two make a great couple. I'm really looking forward to your wedding."

"Me, too! Liz and I were just talking about the flowers, and she's made a list of everything."

"Oh, good. We'll get started early Saturday morning, and by the time the guests arrive, all the flowers will be ready."

"I'm so grateful to you and Liz for taking care of the flowers. It really means a lot to us."

"We're happy to do it. I suppose we'd better move along. We just started our walk, and Goldie's already lying down. Look at them," Fran said. The two dogs had been sitting next to each other while we all talked, but now they were both lying down side by side, snuggled close to one another. "They're so cute. If it were lighter, I'd take their picture. Come on, Goldie," she urged, gently tugging Goldie's leash. "Get up, girl."

Brian insisted on walking me to my door, even though it was only a few yards away from where we were standing on the front sidewalk, and making sure I was safe inside before they left on their walk.

I'd intended to take my cell phone with me to Liz's because I'd been expecting both Cynthia and Tara to get in touch, but when I turned on the kitchen lights, I discovered that I'd left the phone lying on the kitchen counter. I picked it up to check for messages. Sure enough, Tara had left a voice mail letting me know that I could pick up Megan at Lisa's house in the morning. She gave me the address and Megan's phone number so that I could confirm the pickup time with Megan.

When I looked at my texts, the first one I saw was from Megan, letting me know that her grandparents' flight would land around ten in the morning. I texted back, saying I'd pick her up at eight. It took only an hour to drive to Des Moines, but I wanted to allow some extra time, just in case. If their flight arrived on time, we should easily make it back to Center City before noon.

The other text on my phone came from Cynthia. Marcie had contacted her, knew about the emergency board meeting, and promised that she'd be there after extracting a promise from Cynthia that the police wouldn't be waiting for her at FFF's office. Cynthia's message reminded me that I'd meant to ask Wes about the possibility of having his friend, the private investigator, follow Marcie from the meeting at FFF tomorrow afternoon. If we couldn't come to some reasonable agreement with her—a long shot, in my opinion—then we might as well make sure that the police knew where to find her so that they could serve the warrant for her arrest.

I waited up for a while, in case Wes had the time to call me, but when I hadn't heard from him after a couple hours, I went to bed, planning on an early start in the morning. I knew I could rely on Bear to wake me up, which he did promptly at five o'clock.

Even though I groaned as I rolled out of bed, I didn't really mind indulging my dog in a pre-dawn walk, especially since I'd be away from home most of the day.

Bear caught on that something was up when I packed his travel bag with some snacks for him and Goldie, his portable water bowl, and two new stuffed animals, one for each of the dogs. They'd undoubtedly have fun tossing them around, and they'd probably end up shredded, but, in the meantime, they'd be amused.

When I went to the laundry room to grab his collar and leash, Bear pranced around in excitement, and I had to tell him to sit still while I snapped on his leash. He was raring to go when we walked out the front door, and he automatically headed toward Brian and Fran's house. By this time, he knew the drill.

After I dropped Bear off, I returned home and checked the back of my SUV to make sure I hadn't left any class supplies there. I didn't know how much luggage Megan's grandparents would bring, but I wanted to make sure there was as much room as possible. I took my portable vacuum and quickly cleaned up any stray Bear hairs that might be lingering in the back seat.

I'd programmed Lisa's address into the GPS on my phone because I'd never heard the name of her street before, and I had no idea what part of Center City it was in. It was a good thing I left the house a bit early because it turned out that Lisa lived on the other side of town in a neighborhood of old craftsman homes that probably dated from sometime around the early nineteen hundreds.

Every house on her block was well maintained with grassy lawns, shady trees, and pretty flowers in abundance. There wasn't a garage in sight, and several cars were parked on the side of the street where Lisa lived. However, there was some space on the other side of the street, so I circled the block, noticing as I drove around the block that an alley ran in back of the houses.

Curious, I turned into the alley and saw that most of the homeowners had added a garage at some time during the past century, although a few had only a graveled parking space in their backyard for their cars. Driving out of the alley, I turned left, and circled back in the opposite direction, pulling into the vacant spot across the street from Lisa's house.

I looked across the street and saw a man at the door, and I glimpsed Megan as she promptly opened and quickly closed it again. When the man turned, I took a closer look.

If Bear had been with me, he surely would have raised a racket.

It was the same man who had delivered dead black roses to Tracey during my shower!

Chapter 12

He was crossing the street in front of me as I jumped out of my SUV. I wasn't about to waste this opportunity to find out who he was.

"Hey!" I yelled in his direction. "Just a minute!"

Startled, he turned and looked at me, then began running. I ran after him, but since I was wearing flip-flops, I couldn't come close to matching his speed. He disappeared around the corner, and, by the time I reached it, he was nowhere in sight. Down the block, I spotted a black pick-up truck pulling away from the curb. It was too far away for me to be able to read the license plate number.

My pulse racing from my sprint, I walked back toward Lisa's house. If only I'd been able to catch up to the man, I could have found out whether Liam really sent the dead roses to Tracey. Unfortunately, my efforts hadn't accomplished anything. Even if I had accosted him, he might have refused to talk to me. I had the distinct impression that he'd recognized me, though, and I wondered whether he wanted to avoid me in particular or whether he'd have run away from anybody who shouted at him. In any case, he'd wasted no time in dashing away.

Then there was the black pickup truck. Since the nasty incident in the parking lot after Wes and I dined at Tony's a few days ago, I felt paranoid every time I saw a black truck, but I'd also begun to notice that there were lots of them in Center City. I hadn't seen the man get into the truck; he could have gone anywhere by the time I got to the corner and looked down the block.

Back at Lisa's house, Megan opened the front door seconds after I knocked. She flung her arms around me and thanked me for agreeing to drive her to the airport in Des Moines to meet her grandparents' flight from Los Angeles. When she stepped back, I saw a black rolling suitcase with its handle up sitting next to the wall in the foyer. Megan saw me looking at the bag and hastened to explain.

"That's my bag. I'm going to stay with my grandparents at a motel when we get back to town."

"Okay, Megan," I said. "Uh, say, I noticed that a man came to your door a few minutes before I did. Do you know who he is?"

"No clue," she replied. "He delivered flowers. I put them on the table over there." She pointed to an oak library table sitting against the wall. A bouquet of white glads, lilies, and carnations, punctuated with greenery nestled in a low white basket. The tasteful arrangement obviously had been assembled by a professional florist. Could the mystery man really work for a florist? He'd been wearing the same gray shirt and pants he wore when he brought Tracey the dead roses on Saturday. His clothing looked something like a uniform might, but there'd been no emblems on it naming a business or identifying him as an employee of any business. If he did work for a florist, why had he run when I'd called to him? Where was the florist's van? Would a legitimate florist agree to send dead black roses to someone? Pulling a stunt like that wouldn't enhance a business's reputation.

"There wasn't any card, but I didn't notice until after he left, so I have no idea who sent them," Megan told me. "The guy just mumbled 'for you' and 'sorry' and left, like he was in a big hurry."

It was certainly odd that he'd said "sorry." I'd received lots of flowers after my husband's death, but none of the people who delivered them had said "sorry." I also wondered whether he meant that the flowers were for Megan or for the family. Without a card, it was impossible to know who the intended recipient was.

"They're lovely," I said. "If you'd like me to, I can call around to the florists here in town and try to find out who sent them."

"Oh, would you, Laurel? Thanks so much! Aunt Lisa's not going to be happy with me that I didn't notice there wasn't a card. I suppose it must have fallen out of the bouquet."

Megan looked as though she might cry.

"It's all right, Megan," I said, seeking to reassure her. "It's not a big problem, and it's certainly not your fault."

She gulped and nodded, holding back tears. But she didn't say anything.

Setting the lock on the front door, she grabbed the handle of her suitcase, rolled it out onto the front stoop, and turned back, rattling the door handle to make sure the house was locked.

"Aunt Lisa would kill me if I ever left the door unlocked," she said. Realizing how her statement sounded, she hastened to correct it. "I mean she wouldn't like it very much."

Stranger and stranger, I thought, as we crossed the street and I hoisted Megan's suitcase into the back of the SUV. First, there was the mystery of the anonymous delivery guy, and then there was the fact that Lisa's parents weren't going to stay with their daughter while they were in Center City. For that matter, Megan wouldn't be staying at Lisa's anymore, either.

The Morrisons weren't like any other family I knew. I had to admit I was relieved that Megan, rather than Lisa, had greeted me. My last encounter with her had left me speechless. Wes and I had agreed that we really didn't want anything more to do with the woman, and she was definitely on her way out as our real estate agent.

We'd decided the best course for us would be to avoid her completely for the rest of the week. When we returned from our honeymoon, there'd be time enough to fire her and find ourselves a different, more laid-back agent, someone who would actually listen to what we had to say.

Megan sat quietly in the front passenger seat while I maneuvered my way through traffic on the short stretch of highway that led to Interstate 80. Once we turned onto I-80, it would be a straight shot into Des Moines. As usual, much of the traffic on the interstate consisted of lots of long-haul trucks since the highway was a major route running all the way across the country, from the east coast to San Francisco.

The scenery along our route consisted of field upon field of neatly planted rows of corn and soybeans. Now that I'd lived in Iowa for almost four years, I felt embarrassed that I'd thought all those fields of corn were sweet corn when I'd first moved to Iowa, but I soon learned from the natives that the corn growing in the large fields all over the state was anything but sweet. I found out that field corn is mainly used to feed livestock and make ethanol, although some of it ends up in corn flakes, corn syrup, corn meal, corn tortillas, and various other foods.

Sweet corn, on the other hand, was great to eat right off the cob, especially when picked the same day. Liz had educated me on that point a few weeks after I'd moved into my house in Hawkeye Haven when she invited me to go along with her to a friend's place out in the country to pick sweet corn from the friend's garden.

She and her friend had shown me how to remove all the corn silk, peel back and discard the husks, and trim the stalk before popping the ears of corn into a kettle of boiling water for a few minutes. Sweet corn was delicious slathered with butter and sprinkled with salt and pepper.

I was making myself hungry just thinking about it, considering my breakfast had consisted of two cups of coffee and a few sips of orange juice. Since I was dieting, I'd thought it would be a good idea to save some of my precious calorie allotment for lunch. Maybe if we got back to Center City soon enough, Wes might be able to meet me for lunch.

I glanced at Megan, feeling that I should be talking to her, but she hadn't spoken a word since we'd left Lisa's house, and now she was staring, trance-like, out the window, watching the fields go by. In her short pink tee-shirt dress and sandals, she looked about twelve, rather than twenty-one.

"My Aunt Erica's coming tomorrow, but then she has to go back to Switzerland for work in a few days. We're going to have a private service—just the family. I think I'll go home with gram and gramps after mother's funeral. I don't want to stay with Aunt Lisa anymore. We were staying at her house only because of the fire in mom's apartment. I don't think she really wanted us there at all."

Since Megan was probably right on that score, I didn't dispute her assessment of Lisa's attitude. Lisa didn't seem to be concerned with anything but her real estate business, and I assumed that was because she wanted to make a lot of money.

From my observations, I'd say that she'd spent quite a bit. Restoration of a house as old as the one she lived in wouldn't have come cheap, and, if I didn't miss my guess, the oak library table in her foyer was Stickley mission oak dating from the same time as Lisa's house itself. I hadn't seen any of the rooms beyond the foyer, but I wouldn't have been surprised if the rest of the house was furnished in the same arts and crafts style. Period furniture wouldn't come cheap.

"This was the first summer vacation since high school that mom and I could get together. I go to UCLA, and I've taken summer classes every year until now to rack up more credits, but I thought I'd take a break from college this summer. Mom wasn't working as much as she did when she owned her own management company, and she said we'd be able to have some fun, but when I got here, I found out about the fire and having to stay with Aunt Lisa. They didn't get along too well, so it wasn't fun at all. If it weren't for Tara, I probably would have gone back to Los Angeles before now."

So Megan was a college student on summer break, and it didn't sound as though she'd seen much of her mother for some time. In an attempt to get Megan's mind off her troubles for a few minutes, I asked her what she was studying.

"Oh, history," she replied, "but I've changed my major a couple times, and I think I should change it again. I can't do much with a history degree, except teach, and I wouldn't be any good at it. I don't know how you can stand up in front of a whole class of people and talk to them, Laurel. I'd be petrified."

"I've never given it much thought, I guess, but if teaching doesn't appeal to you, of course, you shouldn't do it. What else interests you, beside history?"

"Oh, I don't know. I have no idea what I want to do. I could never be in sales like Aunt Lisa. Someone or other was always getting mad at mother when she owned her property management company, and I wouldn't want to have to deal with angry people. If I could just stay home and read books all day, I'd be happy," she said with a sigh. "I guess that's not a job, though."

"Oh, there's our turn-off. We'll be at the airport in no time."

"We're supposed to pick gram and gramps up by the baggage claim," Megan said. "The last time I checked, their flight was due to land on time. I'll check again."

She pulled her phone from her bag and worked her thumbs busily. I'd never gotten the hang of the thumb maneuvers myself, but I found the speed that some people were able to type with their thumbs amazing

"Still on time," she said. "I hope they're all right. This trip will be so hard on them. I hope the airline met them with wheelchairs like they're supposed to."

"So do I. I thought Tara told me that your grandmother uses a walker. I didn't realize they both need wheelchairs."

"They don't, not for short distances anyway, but both of them have trouble getting around. Gram broke her hip last year, and gramps can't move his arm since he had a stroke. They can walk, but not too far or too fast."

"Okay. Well, I'll park, and we'll go meet them. Once we make sure they're ready with their bags, you can wait with them, while I get the car and come to the passenger pickup area."

Megan nodded, and in a few minutes, we'd parked and were on our way into the airport.

Megan spotted her grandparents immediately and

rushed to them. They were both sitting in wheelchairs, two uniformed airline employees behind them, a folded aluminum walker and two suitcases beside them. Even though I knew they had health problems, their frail appearance shocked me. Mrs. Morrison, with her wispy white hair, deep wrinkles, and spindly limbs, looked as though she might break if Megan hugged her, but I noticed that Megan's embrace was very gentle. It was more robust for her grandfather, who pulled her to him with his right arm, and she leaned over and kissed him on top of his head. He was bald and chubby, with liver spots covering his face and arms. They both looked exhausted from their trip, but they brightened as soon as they saw Megan.

After quick introductions all around, I asked the airline attendants if they could bring the couple to the passenger pickup area when I drove up, and they agreed. I rushed back to my SUV and drove around to the lane reserved for dropping off and picking up passengers. They were waiting at the curb for me. Luckily, I snagged a spot right away. I jumped out and loaded the folded walker and the suitcases in the back while Megan helped her grandmother into the front passenger seat and then settled her grandfather in the back seat, seating herself beside him. Megan reached across him, pulled the seatbelt out, and fastened it for him. It wasn't long before we were headed back to Center City.

When I met the Morrisons at the airport, I'd expressed my condolences. Since we left the airport, Mrs. Morrison hadn't said anything, and I assumed she might not feel like engaging in conversation, so I hadn't tried to talk to her, either, but she broke her silence as soon as we reached Interstate 80.

"Did you know our Patty?" she asked in a tremulous

voice.

"Only slightly," I fudged. "I live in Hawkeye Haven, and she used to be the HOA manager there."

"That awful place!" she said vehemently. "I can't believe they fired her! It wasn't right."

If she only knew how right it was, Patty's mother would have been shocked, but, understandably, Patty hadn't shared the details of her shady practices that had justifiably led to her ousting from Hawkeye Haven. I certainly had no intention of informing Patty's mother of her daughter's malfeasance, so I kept mum.

"She couldn't get a decent job after that," she continued, "until Lisa finally broke down and recommended her as a property manager to the owner of Gold Medal. Patty hated asking Lisa for a favor, but she was desperate. She'd only been working there a little while, finally getting back on her feet, before that terrible fire in her apartment. Now she's left us forever."

The sad reality of her daughter's death probably hadn't hit her full force yet, and she was still struggling to come to terms with it. She reached into her handbag, withdrew a tissue, and dabbed at the tears rolling down her cheeks.

There was really nothing I could say except to repeat that I was sorry for their loss. Mrs. Morrison whispered "thank you," as she crumbled the tissue. Neither Megan nor Mr. Morrison had made a peep since Mrs. Morrison started talking to me. I glanced in the rear-view mirror to check on them and saw that Megan was leaning against her grandfather, and both of them had their eyes closed. I didn't know whether they were sleeping or just resting. If either of them had heard what Mrs. Morrison had said to me, they gave no sign.

"Patty was the apple of our eye," Mrs. Morrison told

me. "She was our youngest. I was forty-five when she was born. Erica and Lisa were quite a bit older—our oldest Erica was old enough to be Patty's mother. So the three of us spoiled Patty, I suppose. She was such a beautiful and talented girl. Everybody loved her."

Well, not everybody. The person Mrs. Morrison had just described didn't sound like the Patty I'd known. But I understood that Mrs. Morrison was relating memories of the past. Patty definitely hadn't kept her mother up to date on her dealings at Hawkeye Haven.

From what Mrs. Morrison had told me, I inferred that Lisa must have been the somewhat-overlooked middle child. With a big sister who spoiled her baby sister and the spoiled child getting most of the family's attention, perhaps Lisa had some reason to resent not only Patty, but also the rest of her family. Poor Megan had suffered some of the unfortunate fallout from the Morrison family dynamics. Of course, I based my speculation on what Mrs. Morrison had said. Others in the family might have a different view of the situation, but I thought her words were telling.

"Are we going to get there soon?" I heard Mr. Morrison ask Megan. "I need to make a pit stop."

"Uh, I'm not sure, Gramps."

"We should be at your motel in about five minutes. We're taking the next exit to Center City. I can stop at the service station right off the ramp, if you like," I said loud enough to be heard in the back seat

"Oh, that's okay. I can wait. I thought it might be a while before we got there."

I stepped on the gas, passed a few big rigs, and was soon merging onto the off-ramp. The two-lane highway we took led to Center City in just a few miles, and their motel was on the outskirts of town. I pulled up under the canopy by the lobby door, and Megan hopped out, went around the car, and assisted her grandfather while Mrs. Morrison and I waited in the car.

In a few minutes, Megan came back and told us that their rooms were on the first floor not far from the lobby, and the shortest way was through the lobby. There weren't any other cars around, so I wasn't blocking the door. I unloaded the suitcases while Megan grabbed the folded walker, pulled it open, and helped her grandmother get out. She gripped the walker and pushed down on it to make sure it was steady before handing it to her grandmother.

"I can get the bags, Megan," I told her as she pulled up the suitcase handles.

"That's okay, Laurel. I can take it from here."

She gave me a hug and said softly, "Thank you so much for driving, Laurel."

"We really appreciate it," her grandmother piped up. "Now where do you suppose Lisa's got to? She was supposed to meet us here."

No sooner had Mrs. Morrison made the comment than a dark gray BMW wheeled into the lot and pulled up under the canopy in back of us.

Lisa put one foot out of the car, stood on her left leg, and waved at her mother.

"Hi, Mom. Clients are waiting for me, so I can't stay."

With that, she sat back down, behind the wheel, and pulled her seat belt on with one hand while she steered the BMW with the other, whipping around my SUV, and exited the motel's parking lot, cutting off another driver in the process.

Chapter 13

Mrs. Morrison watched her daughter's departure, her mouth agape. She shook her head.

"Doesn't have room for us at that house she remodeled and can't even kiss her own mother 'hello,'" she muttered to herself.

"Come on, Gram," Megan urged her. "Gramps is waiting for us."

At least, tending to her grandparents' needs was providing Megan with something useful to do as well as a temporary distraction from her grief.

Hoping that he'd have time to meet me for lunch, I called Wes and was delighted to learn that he did. He suggested Tony's, but I wasn't quite ready to go back to the parking lot where someone had tried to run us down, so we decided to go to a new place that his sister Denise had recommended.

Fifteen minutes later, we were sitting in a cozy booth at the Happy Hamburger. Denise usually went in for a more upscale dining experience, but obviously she liked casual dining as well because that's what the tiny place offered. Even though the place was busy, the high backs of our booth effectively buffered us from the other patrons, and we were able to talk privately.

"I saw the young guy who brought Tracey those dead roses this morning. He was delivering flowers to Lisa's house, and he may have been driving a black pickup, but I'm not sure about that." I proceeded to fill Wes in on all the details about my strange encounter with the delivery man. "Do you suppose he really works for a florist?" I asked.

"Could be, but his moves suggest he doesn't," Wes said thoughtfully. "Why don't you let me check with the local florists? They'll answer an inquiry from the police more readily than one from a member of the public."

"That would be great! What do you make of the black pickup truck? I really don't know if the guy was driving it or not."

"Could be just a coincidence, but my radar's up, too. If he drove that pickup when we were attacked, then it's likely that whoever's after me wants to get at me through you. That would fit in with my theory about an angry relative, someone who blames me for sending a loved one to prison. In that case, I'd read the dead flowers as a warning, but it's cryptic.

"From Tracey's impressions of this delivery man and your description of him, he doesn't sound familiar to me. And since he ran away from you this morning, he may not mean you any harm. I'd really like to get my hands on the guy and find out, once and for all, whether Liam's behind the black roses prank."

"I would, too. Liam seemed believable when he told us he didn't do it, but I guess you never know."

"Right. Like I told you, I can usually tell whether or not a suspect's lying to me, but not Liam. He hasn't called Tracey since we talked to him, has he?"

"No. She would have let you know. He did unfollow her on Facebook, which is a good sign, I guess."

"Or he wants us to think it's a good sign."

"You have such a suspicious mind, Lieutenant Wesson."

"That's my job," he said grinning. "Now, let's see what's on the menu. They have hamburgers and more hamburgers. I'm thinking I'll have a hamburger."

Wes ordered a double bacon cheeseburger with fries, and I ordered a plain turkey burger and a small salad with dressing on the side. Wes didn't notice that my order was a little different from usual until I removed the plain turkey patty and set the bun aside.

"What in the world are you doing?" he asked.

"Oh, uh, nothing," I fibbed. "Maybe I'm not very hungry."

"And maybe you are." He grinned at me. "Don't tell me you're on a diet."

Sheepishly, I admitted that I was.

"But why?" he asked. "I can see that you haven't gained any weight. If anyone's gained a couple pounds, it's me."

"I don't believe it. You always look super," I said, "and you're right. I haven't gained any weight. It's just a precaution. I want to make sure that my wedding gown fits perfectly on Saturday."

"You always look gorgeous."

"I'm glad you think so, but just in case—" I looked longingly at his fries.

"I feel guilty chowing down on this double burger while you're starving," he said.

"No need. It's just for a few days. I don't plan on dieting while we're on our honeymoon."

"Well, okay. But make sure you eat enough to keep up your strength. We wouldn't want you passing out at the wedding."

"Yes, sir!" I said jokingly, as I liberally sprinkled black pepper on my turkey patty.

I told him about my trip to Des Moines and Lisa's brief greeting to her mother. "Even though I've seen her in action before, that really takes the cake," I declared. "She didn't even leave her car to greet her own mother."

"It's hard to believe anyone can be so callous."

"I don't think she gets along very well with her family."

"Even so—"

"Hopefully, we won't see Lisa again before our wedding, but if she should call me, I think I'll go ahead and tell her to forget showing us any more property, if that's okay with you."

"It's fine with me. The captain gave me the name of the agent he used when he bought his new house last year. He assured me that this guy isn't pushy at all, so I thought maybe we could give him a try when we get back."

"That's a good idea. Let's do it," I said, barely dipping a little bite of salad into the dressing I'd requested on the side. Wes's hamburger smelled good, but I tried not to think about it. I only needed to maintain my resolve a few more days until after we said our vows.

"What's on your agenda this afternoon?" Wes asked.

"An emergency meeting of FFF at three this afternoon, and Marcie's the star of the show."

Wes looked up in surprise. "Marcie? You told me that Cynthia saw her Saturday, but this is new. I take it she contacted someone on the board."

"She contacted Cynthia. At first, she said she wanted to come back as FFF's director, but Cynthia told me she backed off that a little, and she thinks maybe we can put together a plan for restitution."

"Or you could have her picked up. I can arrange for some officers to be there with the arrest warrant."

"I know. We thought about that, but Cynthia assured Marcie we wouldn't have the police there waiting for her."

"That wasn't a great idea on Cynthia's part, but I guess since Marcie didn't commit a violent crime, I can understand. The district attorney might agree to a plea deal if there's a plan in place for her to make restitution. It's totally up to him, though. He might want to throw the book at her because she skipped town."

"The thing is, Wes, I doubt that Marcie will be very cooperative. We don't know where she's staying, but I thought maybe if we had her followed, we'd find out, and then she could be served."

"Who's this *we*?"

"Well, I was hoping your private investigator might have time to do it."

Wes laughed. "I thought that's what you were leading up to. I'll give him a call right now. There are several other retired officers who work for him once in a while, so I think the chances are good. Give me the when and where, and I'll check right now. Oh, and do you have a photo of her?"

"I'm sure I do." I pulled my phone out of my handbag. "Yes. Here's one I took at one of our book club meetings. I'll text it to you and you can forward it."

"Consider it done. Now what else can I do for my gorgeous fiancée?"

"Not a thing. You're already calling florists and arranging for Marcie to be followed."

"I'm just a helpful guy," he said with a wink.

"You're the best," I agreed, leaning across the table and giving him a big kiss.

Chapter 14

By the time we left the Happy Hamburger, it was two o'clock. I made a quick call to Fran to check on Bear. He and Goldie were taking an afternoon nap following a strenuous romp with Brian in the backyard, and they'd gone for a long walk in the park in the morning. Fran promised to send me a video of their playtime and told me not to worry about picking Bear up. She could give him dinner if my meeting ran long.

With only an hour until the scheduled emergency board meeting, I decided I might as well head to FFF's offices and wait with Cynthia until the meeting began. I found her in her office, working on a grant proposal.

"Oh, Laurel, I'm glad you're here early. Maybe you could take a look at this draft of our grant proposal and let me know if I need to add anything. I pretty much modeled it on last year's proposal to the Carver Foundation."

"Sure. I'd be happy to take a look."

"Why don't you sit here," Cynthia said, getting up, "and you can read it on the monitor, unless you'd rather read a printed copy."

"No, I'll read it on the computer," I said, sitting in her chair.

"How about some coffee?"

"Love some. Just black."

"I know. Strict diet until the wedding. Come to think of it, you usually take it black, anyway."

While Cynthia bustled off to the tiny break room, I

scanned the document she was preparing.

"Looks like you're done, except for adding last year's figures," I said. "It looks fine to me. FFF should have a good chance of getting this grant again."

"I'm glad you think so. It's the first grant proposal I've written for FFF. Our bookkeeper should have the figures ready for me soon."

We sipped our coffee, and I glanced at the clock. The meeting wasn't due to start for half an hour yet.

"I'm not looking forward to seeing Marcie," I said.

"Neither am I, but she acted a little more reasonable after I promised we wouldn't have the police waiting here for her, so I have some hope that she'll come around. The whole situation's so awkward, especially since she was a member of our book club."

"Yes, it sure is. Say, Cynthia, remember when you mentioned that Marcie didn't own her house in Hawkeye Haven?"

"Sure. That's what Viola told me."

"Viola didn't happen to mention whether Gold Medal Real Estate was involved in the lease agreement or handling the property management, did she?"

"Oh, I don't remember. What's on your mind?"

"It's probably nothing. I don't know why I made the connection, but I was wondering if Patty could have been involved."

"No idea, but I'm sure Viola would tell me. Would you like me to ask her about it?"

"If you don't mind."

"Say no more."

While Cynthia called Viola from the office phone, I went to the break room to refill my mug, but there was hardly any coffee left in the coffee pot, so I rinsed it and brewed a fresh pot.

"Any luck?" I asked Cynthia when I returned to her

office with my mug of steaming coffee.

"Yes, you must be psychic. Viola told me that Gold Medal always handles her property—she owns a couple of other rentals around town, besides the house Marcie was leasing. I also found out that Viola wasn't too happy when Patty took over her account a few months ago. She remembered what a giant pain she was when she managed Hawkeye Haven's HOA. Anyway, Gold Medal's been managing her properties for years, so she decided to stay with them, despite Patty.

"Here's the interesting part: Patty canceled Marcie's lease, because she hadn't paid her rent. This was shortly after Marcie left town, but Marcie contacted Viola a few days ago, claiming that she'd paid every penny on time, and she showed her receipts from money orders. Marcie was furious with Patty and demanded Viola do something about it because she wants to move back into her house."

"That's interesting," I said thoughtfully.

"It sounds like Marcie's planning on staying in Center City. I can't imagine why she's so confident that she's going to skate on the embezzlement charges."

"I don't know, either. It's almost like she's in denial," I said, but what really struck me was Marcie's anger at Patty, according to Cynthia's friend, Viola. Furious enough to do her harm? Lots of Hawkeye Haven residents disliked Patty, but, once she'd been fired, most homeowners were just glad our homeowners' association was under new and more reasonable management. I hadn't heard anyone grousing about Patty for months.

"Here comes Amy." I stood up and waved at Amy.

The FFF director's office was glassed in, so she saw me right away and headed to Cynthia's office, rather than the conference room, where the board met.

"I thought maybe I should get here a little early," Amy said. "Let's go on into the conference room."

We followed Amy to the conference room. Since she was board president now, she sat at the head of the table. Cynthia and I sat on either side of her. At the last emergency board meeting, Amy and Marcie had faced each other from opposite ends of the conference table, and Marcie had tried to stare down Amy, but Amy had never wavered. Marcie had flounced out of the meeting, slamming the door behind her, never showing any remorse for her embezzlement.

I was afraid this meeting might be much the same, although I felt hard-pressed to understand why Marcie would bother meeting with the board if she didn't plan to offer restitution.

By three o'clock the entire board had gathered, but Marcie hadn't shown up yet. I left the conference room and looked outside. FFF's offices are on the second floor of a strip mall, so I scanned the parking lot below for Marcie. I didn't see anyone moving about. I wondered where the private detective had stationed himself and guessed he probably sat in one of the parked cars, waiting for Marcie to make her appearance.

Just as I turned away from the door, I heard someone open it.

"Oh, Laurel, it's you," Marcie said. "You know, if you'd have let me help with the audit in the first place, we wouldn't be in this predicament now."

We weren't in any predicament; Marcie was the one in trouble. The nerve of the woman! She'd offered her help when I'd been tasked with overseeing the audit so that she could cover her tracks. It was a good thing I hadn't fallen for her shady offer, or we'd never have discovered that she'd embezzled money from FFF.

I didn't take the bait, and I ignored her as we walked to the conference room, where she took the seat opposite Amy. She placed a leather portfolio on the table and took out a stack of documents, which she passed around the table, directing each of us to take one. She acted as though she, not Amy, were in charge of the meeting

"What is this?" Amy demanded.

"It's my proposal," Marcie replied. "As you can see, it provides for restoring certain monies to FFF, although I can assure you that there was never anything wrong in the first place. I started this organization, and I was rightfully entitled to compensation."

"Yes, your salary," Roger, our treasurer, said. "You weren't entitled to dip into the till whenever you felt like it."

"My salary was hardly adequate. I believe that was universally acknowledged."

"By whom?" Amy asked. "I certainly never heard any of the board members say you were underpaid. In fact, your salary was higher than most other directors of a charitable organization the same size."

Marcie shrugged. "I dispute that," she said, "but you can't deny that the plan I'm proposing is a good one. You'll get me back as director, and I'll donate some of my salary to FFF. You all know what a great job I did fund-raising. I know more about how to run a campaign than this pretender ever will." She nodded toward Cynthia.

I wondered why Marcie felt the need to take a dig at Cynthia. I suppose Marcie would have resented anyone who took her place, but Cynthia hadn't appointed herself as temporary director of FFF. That had been the board's decision. It didn't seem like a very good strategy, either. I thought the old saying about catching more flies with honey might apply in this situation.

I glanced at Marcie's proposal, and it was plain to see that she wanted to come back as director at a higher salary, "donate" a tiny fraction of her salary to FFF each pay period, have the board inform the district attorney that we'd reached a restitution agreement with her, and ask him to drop the charges against Marcie. Since the district attorney made his own decisions about prosecutions, anything the board had to say would be merely a suggestion; we couldn't tell him to do anything.

"You do realize that we can't tell the district attorney what to do?" Roger asked.

"You can urge him to drop the charges," Marcie said. "You play golf with him, don't you? Use your influence."

"Well, I don't know about that."

"Let's stop right there," Amy said. "I think the board needs to discuss this without Marcie present."

"But I should be here," Marcie protested.

"You're no longer a board member or an employee of FFF, so you're not entitled to be here for the rest of the meeting. We've received your proposal, and we'll let you know what we decide."

"Move to allow Marcie to stay and participate in our discussion," said Dorothy, a long-time board member.

A second to Dorothy's motion followed quickly, forcing a vote on the motion.

"All in favor of allowing Marcie to stay and participate in our discussion about her proposal?" Three hands went up, including, surprisingly, Roger's. "All opposed?" Four of us raised our hands. "The motion is defeated," Amy announced. "Marcie, we'll let you know what we decide. I suppose, since you won't give us your phone number or address, you'll have to check with me later."

Marcie had no choice but to leave. I couldn't believe that three of the board members had voted in favor of the motion. As treasurer, Roger had been more shocked than anyone when we'd first uncovered Marcie's embezzlement. Although he had tried to put together a plan to get her a new job out of state and re-pay FFF, she'd refused to listen to him last time.

As a non-voting member of the board, Cynthia was entitled to put her two cents worth in, but she'd refrained from commenting, probably feeling that it might be a conflict of interest, even though she'd never sought her job as temporary director. Amy and I had had to convince her that she'd make a great director. Her skills at organization and her efficiency were almost legendary at Hawkeye Haven. She agreed to take the job with the proviso that it be temporary and she'd insisted on the title of temporary director, rather than director.

A heated discussion among the voting members followed Marcie's departure. Predictably, the two members who'd favored letting Marcie stay wanted to accept her proposal. Roger was on the fence, while Amy and I, along with a couple of other board members, were opposed to letting Marcie come back. After a while, I could tell that Roger was changing his stance, but the two opposed hadn't budged from their views. Since it seemed counter-productive to continue to debate, I moved for a vote, and Roger seconded my motion. We turned down Marcie's proposal by a five-to-two margin, and Amy adjourned the meeting.

Cynthia, Amy, and I gathered in Cynthia's office for a quick re-hash, but there wasn't much to say. Marcie would not be returning to FFF, and that was that. Our consensus was that she'd had plenty of nerve to make the attempt.

Now that her status was settled, hopefully once and for all, we agreed that we should go ahead with our plan to let the police know she was in town so that they could serve her with the warrant for her arrest on the embezzlement charges the district attorney had filed when we first brought her crime to his attention several months ago.

If Wes's private eye or one of his associates had been successful in following Marcie home from the board meeting, he would be in touch soon. I put my phone on Cynthia's desk so that I wouldn't miss a call or text message. We waited, chit-chatting about my wedding, a golf tournament Cynthia was playing in on Sunday, and Amy's upcoming dance competition. An hour passed, and we were beginning to wonder whether the investigator had lost Marcie's trail when finally my phone chimed, signaling a new text message.

"This is it!" I exclaimed. "Here's her address. Oh, I don't believe it!"

"What is it, Laurel?" Amy asked.

"The investigator tracked her to 2132 Maquoketa."

Amy and Cynthia both looked at me quizzically. The address meant nothing to them.

"That's the address of the house Wes and I were scheduled to look at Sunday—the same place where Patty drowned!"

Chapter 15

"You're kidding," Amy said. "I thought you told me the house was vacant."

"You're right. There was a lock box on the door—you know, the kind real estate agents use to store keys to vacant properties."

"Maybe the real estate company is renting it to Marcie while they're trying to sell it," Cynthia speculated.

"I guess that must be the case. The private investigator says Marcie let herself in. I'm going to text him and ask him how she did that since I know there was a lock box on the front door when Wes and I went to look at the house on Sunday."

His answer came back in less than a minute. Marcie had used an access key card to open the lock box. According to Wes's PI, most of the local real estate companies used lock boxes with key cards now, and each agent had his or her own card. I supposed Gold Medal Real Estate wouldn't necessarily remove the lock box because a temporary renter had moved in. After all, the property was still listed for sale, and agents would need to show the house to prospective buyers. Even so, I couldn't think of a good reason that the company would have furnished Marcie a lock box key card since it could be used to open lock boxes at other properties that were for sale.

The private investigator had already notified Wes of Marcie's address so that he could pass it along to the officers who would serve the warrant and arrest Marcie. She'd be out on bail in no time, but maybe a short stay at the county jail would jolt her out of fantasyland into reality, bringing her to her senses so that she realized she'd done something wrong.

Wes had warned me that the warrant might not be served immediately, though, and that possibly only a few attempts would be made to serve it. There wasn't the urgency attached to arresting Marcie that there would have been had she committed a violent crime. According to Wes, many people wanted on outstanding warrants were caught when the police ran their license plates after a traffic stop.

Leaving Cynthia to finish her grant proposal, Amy and I left FFF's offices. Amy was on her way to dance rehearsal, and I was headed home. After I parked in my garage, I went to Fran and Brian's house to pick up Bear. Both he and Goldie greeted me joyfully, pausing just long enough for me to pet them before dancing around me as Fran and I slowly made our way back to the kitchen to retrieve the bag I'd brought this morning.

"I didn't feed them dinner yet," Fran said, "but I can tell they're both getting anxious."

"That'll be first on our schedule as soon as we get home, won't it, Bear?" He panted excitedly, and I'm sure he knew exactly what I meant. Bear would never let me forget about feeding him. He seemed to have an internal alarm clock that went off a few minutes before his regular dinnertime.

"Oops! I forgot to send you the video that I took earlier," Fran said, grabbing her phone. "I'm sending it to you now."

"You always take such great pictures, Fran," I said. "Mine never look as good as yours, and whenever I try to shoot a video of Bear, he doesn't cooperate. You really have the knack."

"Thanks, Laurel. I enjoy it."

We heard the garage door open, and Brian came in, carrying a large bag from Foster's.

"Something smells good," I said.

"We didn't feel like cooking tonight, so Brian went to Foster's deli."

"Everything looked good, so I may have gone a little bit overboard," Brian said, as he set the bag down on the counter. "We have plenty of food here, Laurel. Why don't you stay and have dinner with us, unless you have other plans."

"Thanks, Brian. I appreciate the offer, but Tracey's coming over so we can finalize the menu for the wedding luncheon."

"Okay. We'll see you at the wedding, if not before," Brian said cheerfully, as Bear and I departed. A few steps down their sidewalk, I turned to wave at Fran and Brian, who stood together at their front door, holding Goldie back. The two retrievers looked at each other, lifted their heads, and gave each other a farewell bark.

As soon as we entered the house, Bear ran to his food bowl and stood beside it expectantly. I dished out his meal and filled his other bowl with fresh water while he made short work of his dinner. My turkey patty and lunch salad hadn't done much to satisfy my appetite, and I felt half-starved as I pulled a frozen diet dinner out of the freezer and put it into the microwave. No wonder so many dieters gave up so quickly. They were hungry! Only three more days of dieting for me, and I'd be more than happy to put my dieting behind me. I kept telling myself it would be worth it on the Big Day, which was getting closer by the minute.

While I nuked my paltry dinner, I held up my left hand to the light and moved it back and forth, just to watch the diamonds in my engagement ring twinkle. I'd made earrings of dainty rose gold chain interspersed with little Swarovski crystals to wear to the wedding. I hadn't yet decided whether to wear a necklace or not. Right at the moment, I was leaning toward *not*, but I wanted to ask Tracey's opinion when she came over later.

After I ate my meager dinner, I went outside with Bear while he patrolled the perimeter of the backyard. The towel I'd used to dry him after he climbed out of Liz's pool yesterday was still hanging on the wall. While he wandered around, I took it inside and popped it into the washing machine, along with a few other towels, and started the wash cycle. Bear began to bark, so I figured he was ready to come back into the house, but when I went to the patio door to let him in, I saw what the ruckus was all about.

A large calico cat, half-hidden by the leaves of my lilac bush, was perched on the back wall. Bear had run to the wall and was standing on his back legs, his big front paws pressed against the wall. Even though he was a big boy, Bear couldn't reach the cat, but that didn't stop him from barking furiously at it. Extending its paw in a playful batting motion toward Bear, the cat, just out of Bear's reach, appeared to be enjoying Bear's predicament.

I started walking toward the pair, and the calico kitty quickly took off, running gracefully on top of the wall until it leaped off into a neighbor's yard. Satisfied that his nemesis had departed, Bear continued his perimeter patrol, stopping occasionally to roll in the grass, which was higher than usual. Since my dad insisted he wanted to mow it for me on Friday, I hadn't touched it for a week.

I was still wondering how Marcie came to live in the

house at 2132 Maquoketa and why she had a key card that only a real estate agent should have when Bear's ears perked up, and, tail wagging, he ran to the gate.

"Let's go open the door for Tracey," I said, and he ran to the patio door and shot inside, ahead of me. He was waiting at the front door for me to let Tracey in by the time I got to the foyer. I opened the door for her, and Bear raced to the kitchen as soon as she'd petted him.

"My predictable buddy," Tracey said, as we followed Bear to the kitchen. "He's trolling for his treat."

"And I know he won't be disappointed," I said.

"He sure won't. I made him some tuna-rice balls, and I know he'll love them." Tracey removed a plastic container from her huge tote bag and set it on the counter, while Bear brushed against her legs and looked up at her in anticipation.

"Here you go, Bear," Tracey said, putting one treat in Bear's bowl. He snarfed it down, licked his chops, and looked at Tracey expectantly.

"How many more should I give him?" Tracey asked.

"I guess he can have a couple more. Then we'd better cut him off. He'd eat every treat in the container if we let him."

"Okay. Here, Bear. That's all, boy." Tracey dropped two more tuna-rice balls, one at a time, in Bear's bowl before quickly snapping the lid on the plastic container and putting it into the refrigerator.

"Now that's a bare refrigerator, if I ever saw one," she said. "How's the diet going?"

"Fine, which means I feel starved, but I guess I'll survive. Only three more days of dieting, and then I can eat. I hope you've already had dinner."

"I have, but won't going over our menu for Saturday make you feel even hungrier?"

"Probably, but I can put the kettle on. Maybe some hot tea will help. Would you like some?"

"Sure."

After I made the tea, Tracey spooned some sugar into hers, but I refrained, and we settled down in the den and reviewed the menu. Everything Tracey had planned sounded delicious. Since our moms were planning on helping her make the food, all the work wouldn't fall on Tracey. They'd prepare what they could ahead of time at Tracey's house on Friday afternoon. Friday evening we'd all attend a dinner at Denise's house. On the Big Day, they'd finish their preparations and set up the luncheon as a buffet at my house.

Tracey asked me whether I'd like to add or change any items, but I thought the menu looked fabulous, just the way she'd planned it. She tucked her notes away in her tote while I thanked her again for doing double duty as both maid of honor and chef.

"I can't believe I forgot to ask you what happened with Marcie," Tracey said. Although Tracey wasn't a board member of FFF, she knew Marcie from our book club.

"She wants to come back as director," I said.

"That's crazy! After she stole money from FFF, she wants to have another shot at it?"

"Evidently. The majority of the board voted 'no' to her proposal, but a couple of members actually voted for her to return as director. Anyway, she's supposed to contact someone, probably Cynthia or Amy, to find out how the board voted. In the meantime, I arranged—or I should say Wes arranged—for a private detective to follow her after the board meeting."

After I told Tracey where Marcie went after the meeting, I had a light-bulb moment. "What if we cruise by 2132 Maquoketa and see what's happening?" I suggested.

"I can see the wheels turning now," Tracey said. "What are we waiting for? Let's go!"

Before we had a chance to act on my impulsive idea, my phone rang. When I saw the name on my caller ID, I shifted my thinking.

"It's Lisa," I whispered to Tracey. Then I laughed at myself for whispering. Nobody was around to hear what we said.

"Hello," I said brightly, temporarily suspending my intention to tell Lisa that we didn't want her to show us any more houses—ever.

Never one given to idle chit-chat, Lisa launched right into her sales pitch. "I've just this minute listed the perfect house for you and Wes," she gushed. "You're going to want to see this one before anyone else has the chance to look at it. I can show it to you at two tomorrow afternoon."

"Well, uh, I would have to check with Wes. He has to work tomorrow," I said, not pausing long enough for her to respond, "but I have a question for you. Is Gold Medal renting the property at 2132 Maquoketa?"

"I wouldn't recommend renting. Why in the world would you consider leasing, instead of buying?"

"But is it available for rent?"

"No. It's for sale. The owner's already moved to Texas, and he doesn't want to rent it. He's looking for a quick sale. I can negotiate price with him. I'm sure he'd consider an offer substantially below the asking price. He's anxious to sell."

"So nobody's living in the house now?"

"No! I just told you—the owner's left the state." Lisa's exasperation was plain enough. "What's this all about, Laurel?"

"Evidently, someone is staying at that house."

"Don't be ridiculous! It has a lock box. Only authorized real estate agents have a lock box key card."

"Someone saw a woman entering the house with a key card to the lock box."

"So what? There's nothing unusual about that. It must have been an agent checking the place out before she showed it to clients."

"This woman is no agent."

"Then she couldn't possibly have a key card! Honestly, Laurel, you must be so involved in your wedding plans that you're not thinking straight. Let me know if you and Wes want to see my new listing." Although Lisa hung up without waiting for my response, at least I'd learned that Marcie wasn't renting the house at 2132 Maquoketa. She'd obtained the key card from someone, though. According to Lisa, that someone must be a real estate agent.

I'd set my phone on the speaker function before I'd answered Lisa's call so that Tracey would be able to hear every word.

"That's weird," she commented. "How do you suppose Marcie got that key card?"

"I'm not sure," I said slowly, "but I have an idea, and I'd better call Wes so that he can check on it." I poked the speed dial on my phone, and Wes picked up immediately.

"Hey, beautiful! Shall we get hitched Saturday?" he asked cheerfully.

"Of course, since you put it so persuasively," I teased. "Seriously, though, I've just learned something odd, and I wonder if you could possibly check on it."

"Your wish is my command," Wes said. I could picture his grin even though I couldn't see him.

"Something very strange is going on, and I don't know whether it's connected to Patty's death or not, but it may be."

"Go on."

"Marcie Nolan's staying at the house where Patty died. Our private investigator saw her unlock the lock box with a key card and go inside. Lisa happened to call me a few minutes ago, and I asked her whether the house had been rented. It hasn't. She told me that nobody, except a real estate agent, has those access cards for the lock boxes that they use when a house is vacant. What if she took the card from Patty? Maybe she's the one who strangled Patty! Lieutenant Walker has Patty's handbag in evidence. Was her lock box key card in it, or is it missing?"

"Whoa! Slow down, sweetheart. It does sound as though Marcie's squatting at the house, but that doesn't mean that she killed Patty. What would be her motive?"

"Cynthia told me that Marcie was furious with Patty because Patty canceled Marcie's lease. Supposedly, Marcie had kept up her payments for the house she was renting here in Hawkeye Haven, even after she left town a few months ago, but Patty claimed the payments hadn't been made."

"Well, that seems a little thin on the motive, but I've seen thinner. Where did Cynthia get her information?"

"From her friend Viola, who owns the house Marcie was renting. She told Cynthia that Gold Medal manages her rental properties."

"Your network never ceases to amaze me," Wes said mildly. "I'll give the information to Walker, although he probably won't be too grateful. He doesn't like it when anybody else shows an interest in one of his cases."

"Would his attitude prevent him from looking into it?"

"No, but he won't be happy. Anyway, that's his problem. In the meantime, I hope you're not thinking about confronting Marcie. If she's mixed up in Patty's death, she's dangerous."

"Of course not, sweetie," I said. "I have no intention of trying to get in touch with her. She was supposed to call to check on the vote of the board, but I'm sure she'll call Cynthia or Amy. I'm not expecting so much as a phone call from her."

"Okay. That's good. It may be that the warrant's already been served and she's been picked up, but I don't know, so take care. You've had more than your share of danger this week."

"I will. Really, I will," I said earnestly, regretting my earlier hasty impulse to drive over to 2132 Maquoketa to try to find out what Marcie was up to.

After I hung up, Tracey looked at me in amazement.

"Weren't we just ready to walk out the door to track down Marcie? I can't believe you told Wes that you didn't plan to confront her."

"A woman can change her mind, can't she? I really did mean it when I told Wes I wouldn't contact her because I realized when we were talking that Wes is right—she could be extremely dangerous. I want to make it to my wedding in one piece!"

"All right. I guess we both got caught up in the moment. It's a good thing Lisa called when she did. I don't suppose Wes will tell you what he finds out."

"Probably not, not unless it's a matter of public record like, say, Marcie's arrested."

"Do you really think she's responsible for Patty's death? I can't picture her as a murderer, but then I was really shocked when you found out she embezzled all that money from FFF. I guess you never can tell about people."

"I don't know. As Wes said, her motive's not the strongest, but it's just really odd that she has a key card to the property where Patty was killed."

.

Chapter 16

Tracey and I never did get around to discussing whether or not I should wear a necklace with my wedding gown, but I was still leaning toward skipping a necklace. I was afraid that my mother would want me to wear my great-grandmother's pearls. Although they were the real deal and very lovely, I didn't think they'd be a good complement to my dress. Even so, if my mother had her heart set on my wearing the pearls, I'd do it, just to please her.

Not surprisingly, Wes hadn't divulged any new information about Marcie's status, even though we'd talked after Tracey had gone home and again early the next morning, while Bear and I were taking our daily walk. I figured there was nothing he could tell me yet, which probably meant that Marcie hadn't been apprehended. I knew he'd never tell me whether Walker had found the real estate key card in Patty's handbag, where it should have been. It was also possible that, since Walker, not Wes, was in charge of the investigation into Patty's homicide, Walker may not have shared any information with Wes.

Since my parents, Aunt Ellen, and Uncle Bill would be arriving on an afternoon flight from Seattle the next day, I wanted to make sure everything would be ready for them. Aunt Ellen and Uncle Bill would stay with Tracey, and my parents would stay with me. My parents had insisted that I sleep in my own bed the two nights before the wedding, saying they didn't mind sleeping on the sofa bed in the den. I'd slept on it several times when they were visiting, and it wasn't bad, but I didn't think it was nearly as comfortable as my own bed. After they arrived, I would try to persuade them again to use my bedroom.

I took the cushions off the sofa in the den, pulled out the sofa bed, and put sheets on it. Then I started a load of laundry, and tidied the living room and den where I'd left some mail, mainly old advertisements, and a few books lying on the end tables. I dusted, mopped, vacuumed, and cleaned the bathrooms. I was sure my dad would want to use my computer during the visit, so I cleared my desk in the office and set my project notes for my *DIY Bridal Crafts* book on top of my file cabinet so that they would be out of his way. In my craft room, I left all my projects in place. My mother enjoyed sewing about as much as I enjoyed cooking. Since she wasn't into crafts and could barely sew on a button, it was unlikely that she'd darken the doorway of the craft room.

By mid-morning, I was satisfied with my progress. I planned to give the house a quick going-over again tomorrow, before Tracey and I left for the airport in Des Moines to pick up our parents. I poured myself a cup of black coffee and went outside with Bear to sit on the patio for a few minutes. I'd learned that drinking hot tea or coffee helped stave off the hunger pangs. Lunch was two hours away, but I was already looking forward to having my diet meal of cottage cheese, fruit, and salad.

While I drank my coffee, Bear lay down in front of me, his chin on his hard rubber ball, and waited impatiently. He was eager for me to play fetch with him, so I didn't dawdle. When I'd finished, I set my mug on a little side table next to my cell phone, picked up the ball, and heaved it into the far corner of the backyard. Bear leaped up and ran after it. When he returned, holding the ball in his mouth, he whipped his head in my direction, and the ball flew past me onto the patio. It was a rare occasion that I actually caught the ball when he threw it to me, although I'd managed to catch it a couple of times. After I retrieved the ball, I tricked Bear, who had already moved to the back wall in anticipation of a long throw, and gently lobbed the ball only a few yards away from where I was standing. Bear galloped toward it, swooped it up, and trotted to me, nudging my hand with the ball. Then he teased me by hanging onto the ball so that I had to wrest it from his mouth. Panting from the heat of the rapidly warming day, he waited by my side this time while I threw the ball back out onto the lawn. Then when he fetched his ball, he came back to me and dropped it at my feet.

As I stooped to pick it up, my cell phone rang. I threw the ball again for Bear with my right hand and picked up my phone with my left hand. Although I didn't recognize the number, it was a local one, so I decided to answer.

"Hello."

"Laurel, it's Liam."

What could I say? Wes had warned Liam not to call Tracey, but he hadn't cautioned Liam not to call me. I opted for courtesy. Liam had sounded sincere when he'd promised not to contact Tracey.

"Hi, Liam. How are you?"

"How do you think I am after your boyfriend accused me of something I didn't do?" Now he sounded bitter. Maybe I shouldn't have picked up the phone, after all. He quickly relented, though. "I'm sorry, Laurel. I'm not angry with you. I'm not even angry at what's-his-name."

"Wes."

"Wes. I'm not even angry at Wes. I realize he was just trying to protect Tracey, but to threaten to tell my boss—that's beyond the pale, because I didn't do anything wrong."

That was his interpretation. Tracey certainly had a different one. She felt that Liam had been harassing her.

I thought about what he said. He continued, "At first, I couldn't believe that Tracey thought I was harassing her because I kept asking her for dates. I really thought she was joking around with me. I guess I'm not as tuned in as I thought I was, but I promised I wouldn't contact her, so I haven't. I owe her an apology, though, and that's the reason I'm calling you. Please tell Tracey that I'm sorry I didn't realize that she meant what she said. I know that sounds lame, but it's the truth. I joke around so much that I assume everybody else does the same. Could you give her the message? And call off your boyfriend?"

"I'll tell Tracey what you said, Liam. As far as calling off Wes, I don't tell him what to do. As long as you keep your word, you have nothing to worry about."

"Thanks, Laurel."

"One more thing, Liam. Did you send those dead roses to Tracey? I have to know."

"No!" he said emphatically. "I already told you I don't know anything about that. I guess I can understand why Tracey thought it was one of my pranks, considering that she felt I was already annoying her, but I really didn't send them. Cross my heart!"

"I want to believe you, Liam."

"Believe me! I'm telling you the truth! I need this job, Laurel, and I don't need any trouble. My boss has had it in for me ever since I came back here from Florida. I don't know why, but he's constantly on my case. He's looking for any excuse to fire me, but I do my job, and he can't fire me for no reason. It's a long process to fire an employee with this company, but that doesn't mean it can't be done. And he would do it, too. If he could find a reason that his boss and the human resources department would buy into, I'd be gone in a heartbeat."

"Okay, Liam. So long as you keep your word, Wes said that he wouldn't involve your boss."

"But how do I know I'm not going to get the blame for something else I didn't do? Somebody sent Tracey the black roses. What if he does it again?"

"I don't know. I suppose Wes might question you. Look, I'm not too comfortable being the go-between. I'll pass along your apology to Tracey, and you're welcome to talk with Wes directly about your concerns, but I'm not going to relay any more messages to either one of them."

I realized that if Liam hadn't sent Tracey the dead flowers, I might have been a little bit hard on him, but, on the other hand, he'd behaved so aggressively toward Tracey in the weeks before the flower delivery that she'd immediately thought Liam had sent the ugly bouquet.

"Okay. I get it. Thanks for telling Tracey that I'm sorry." Liam definitely did not sound like a happy camper. I wondered whether he would have called me to ask me to convey his apology if he hadn't felt his job might be in jeopardy. It seemed unlikely that his boss would be "out to get" him for no reason, but since I had only Liam's side of the story, there was no way to know his situation at work

Normally, I avoided calling Tracey at work. With her busy schedule and high-pressure job, she didn't need any interruptions, but I thought I should let her know what Liam had said.

I called and left a voice message for her. After about ten minutes, she called me back.

"I was in a meeting when you called. What's up?"

I filled her in on everything Liam had told me. "Do you think he means what he says?" I asked.

"Wow! Liam actually apologized? That's a first. I think maybe he does mean it."

"He wouldn't just be doing it because he thinks Wes might say something to his boss, would he?"

"I doubt it although it's weird he's so concerned about his job. He was kind of the golden boy when he worked at the hospital before. He was always very happy-go-lucky, and he loved to play pranks. When he came back, he seemed different. He was really pushy with me and kept calling me, day and night, after I asked him not to. He just wouldn't take 'no' for an answer; that's why I thought he sent me the black roses. Anyway, nobody's bothered me since Saturday, and Liam hasn't contacted me directly, so I'm not going to give it any more thought. We have more important things to think about, like your wedding. I'm taking tomorrow afternoon off. I can drive us to Des Moines so you won't have to stuff everybody into your SUV."

Tracey's SUV was a lot bigger than mine, and six people could easily fit into it, whereas mine has room for only five, and it would be a crunch, at that. My mom and Aunt Ellen never skimped on luggage, so there were sure to be several large suitcases to transport, too, and my cargo area didn't hold nearly as much as Tracey's. Originally, we'd thought that Tracey would have to stay at work all day Thursday, but I was glad to hear her plans had changed.

"Great! What time do you want to leave?"

"Probably around two o'clock, assuming their

flight's on time."

"All right. Sounds good."

"I'd better get back to it. I want to get as much done as I can before I leave work tomorrow. I'm afraid I'll probably get some phone calls from my team while I'm out, but I'm taking Friday and Monday off, no matter what. See you tomorrow!"

Next on my morning agenda was a trip to the supermarket. Much as I hated to go, I couldn't leave my pantry in its current barren state when my parents would be arriving tomorrow. If I went to Foster's, I'd be tempted by the incredible deli and the mouth-watering selection at the bakery, so I decided to head to the closest big chain supermarket, where the deli and bakery weren't nearly as enticing as those at Foster's. I made my shopping list and vowed to stick to it. Since Tracey was taking care of all the food for the luncheon and she had very specific ideas about what to buy and where to buy it, all I needed was food for my parents' short stay.

After I finished my shopping list, I bade Bear good-bye, promising I'd return shortly. He looked at me with sad eyes, as I petted him and told him to be a good boy. I had to admit that I was a wee bit worried about leaving Bear for eight days while Wes and I were on our honeymoon, but I knew he'd have the best of care, first from my parents, and then from Fran and Brian, after my parents returned to Seattle. Still, I knew he'd miss me, and I'd miss him, too.

I was beginning to feel a bit nervous about my upcoming nuptials. I loved Wes and wanted to marry him, but the events of the past few days had shaken me. My fear of losing Wes, as I'd lost Tim, had been floating around my brain, bubbling up more frequently, even though I'd tried to set my mind on other concerns.

Wes and I had agreed that we should concentrate on enjoying our days together, but my nagging worry kept cropping up. Did all cops' wives experience these fears? I knew mine came from the deep hurt of losing Tim so unexpectedly. I didn't want that hurt to turn me into a nagging wife after I married Wes. Sometimes I just wanted to hold Wes and never let him go, but I didn't want to turn into a clinging wife, either. I sighed.

Only Tracey knew the true depth of my fear. My eyes filled with tears as I thought about how she'd been with me every step of the way after Tim died. For the past five years, she had comforted me when I mourned, encouraged me to pursue my DIY business full-time, persuaded me to move to Hawkeye Haven for a fresh start, and convinced me that the time was right for me to embark on a new relationship when Wes had first shown an interest in me. I knew that, if she were sitting beside me right now, she'd tell me to look forward, not backward.

SuperDuper didn't look busy as I pulled into the parking lot and snagged a spot right in front of the store. I pulled a tissue out of my handbag and quickly dabbed my eyes, resolving to stop dwelling on negative thoughts. I couldn't control the world around me, much as I might want to. I could only hope for the best and love Wes. I didn't doubt that he was the right man for me.

Shopping list in hand, I reached for the door handle, only to start when my phone began playing "Endless Love." I'd almost forgotten that I'd changed my ring tone only a few hours ago.

"Hi, sweetheart. I'm up to my eyeballs here, and I can't tell you much, but watch the local noon news for a breaking story."

"What is it, Wes? Can't you tell me more than that?"

"I can tell you one thing because it's a matter of public record now. Marcie was picked up last night, and she's already out on bail."

"Details?"

"Sorry. That's all I can say about it. I have to run now, but watch the news."

I dropped my cell phone back into my handbag. I knew Wes was telling me all he could, but it was maddening not to know any specifics. Was the noon broadcast about Marcie's arrest? It didn't seem like that would garner a lead news story on any of the local television channels. I'd definitely be tuning in to find out the latest scoop.

I jumped out, pushed the button on my remote to lock the car, and grabbed a stray shopping cart that someone had left in the parking space next to mine. As I entered SuperDuper with my head down, scanning my shopping list, I heard someone call my name. I looked up, and Tara smiled at me.

"Laurel, I'm glad I ran into you," she said. "I wanted to thank you again for driving Megan to Des Moines to pick up her grandparents. Even though she'd told me about their health problems, I didn't really realize how frail they were until I met them last night."

"You visited them at the motel?"

"No, I invited them over for dinner; Lisa brought them over."

"I'm surprised she could find the time. She called me last evening and insisted that Wes and I look at a house this afternoon. Needless to say, we have no intention of doing so. She never stops trying to make a sale."

"No, she doesn't. Even though she dropped off her parents and niece, she claimed that she didn't have time to have dinner with us. I drove them all back to the motel later. I don't know what the story is there, but her behavior definitely isn't normal."

"Well, I may have picked up on what caused some of the problem, but it's only a guess on my part. When we were coming back to Center City, Mrs. Morrison sat in the front with me. She told me that Patty was their favorite daughter, only not in those exact words. From what she said, their oldest daughter Erika doted on Patty, too. I got the feeling that Lisa was pretty much overlooked, and that everything revolved around Patty."

"That would explain some things, all right, but I'm still hard-pressed to understand how Lisa can treat her parents as badly as she does. When she dropped them off at my house, I went outside to greet them, and Lisa didn't even get out of the car to help her mother come up the front porch steps. I helped her while Megan helped her grandfather, and Lisa didn't bother to wait to see that they got inside safely. It certainly sounds as though she felt jealous of Patty. I hate to say it, but maybe she doesn't care that Patty's dead."

"Poor Megan, having to deal with Lisa's behavior on top of her mother's death."

"Yes. On the plus side, Megan seems quite close to her grandparents, and I know she's close to her Aunt Erica, too."

"I think she told me Erica's arriving tomorrow."

"So I understand. She's planning on renting a car at the airport, so that will help. The family won't have to depend on Lisa to drive them around. They're going to have a private service—family only—for Patty on Friday, and they're all leaving the next day. When they go back to California, Megan's going to stay with her grandparents for a while. I hope Lisa shows up for the service, at least."

After Tara left, I looked at my grocery list again and started down the first aisle, thinking about Lisa and her strained relationship with her family.

Lisa didn't appear to care that her sister had died. She'd been jealous of her, and, based on what Mrs. Morrison had told me, she hadn't much wanted to help Patty when she'd needed to find a new job. With Patty's working for Gold Medal, the same real estate agency as Lisa, maybe old resentments Lisa had harbored for years overwhelmed her. Clearly, Lisa behaved in a highly competitive manner, and she'd been unsuccessful competing with her baby sister in the past. As far as I knew, Lisa was the only person who'd known that Patty would be at 2132 Maquoketa on Sunday afternoon. Perhaps she decided to eliminate the competition permanently.

I hurried through the rest of the store, grabbing items from my list. I'd tried to be efficient and make my list out in the same order as the groceries were shelved, but just when I thought I'd finished and was heading to the nearest checkout line, I realized that I'd forgotten to list my father's favorite cereal, so I turned back to the breakfast aisle and added a box of oatmeal. I knew he wouldn't eat it without brown sugar, so I returned to the aisle with all the baking ingredients and bought a bag of brown sugar, too.

Finally satisfied that I had everything I needed, I returned to the front of the store and found customers lined up. It looked as though most of the checkers had decided to take their breaks at the same time. The lone checker was quickly scanning and bagging items with one hand while holding a microphone in the other and calling for help to the checkout area. I hoped some more checkers would show up soon because I wanted to get home in time to watch the news at noon. In a few minutes, a couple checkers appeared, and three lines now formed. I'd moved to a different line in the hope of getting out of the store more quickly, but the line I was in ended up being the slowest of the three; the man in front of me couldn't find his credit card when it came time for him to pay his bill. After looking through his wallet a couple of times for the missing card, he came up empty. Then he began searching his pockets for cash. He was five dollars short, so he asked the checker to hold his order while he went next door to the bank to get some more money. I dug a five-dollar bill out of my purse and offered to pay the difference, but the man insisted he would go to the bank. As he departed, the checker had to void the bill for his order and put it aside before she could check out my groceries. I bagged them and put them in my cart as fast as she scanned them, hurriedly paid, and rushed out of the store.

Pulling into my garage with less than a minute to spare, I left the groceries in my SUV, greeted Bear, pacified him with a few baby carrots, and turned on the television, tuning it to one of the local stations.

I shouldn't have worried, though. After a sunny greeting from the news anchor about what great weather we could expect for the next few days, a commercial appeared. I had enough time to bring the groceries in and stow the milk, salad greens, and fruit in the refrigerator before the news began, but since the broadcast started with national news headlines, I had to wait for the local news, anyway.

Finally, the story I'd been waiting for came on.

"Police may have caught a break in their investigation into the murder of a local real estate agent," the announcer stated. "We'll be right back in a moment with details."

Chapter 17

The news program cut to a commercial, this one advertising a sale on mattresses at a local furniture store. Another commercial followed, this time for an attorney representing personal injury claimants. I waited impatiently for the news anchor to pop back on the screen. By the time he re-appeared, it had been only a couple of minutes, but it seemed like much longer.

He recounted the basic facts about Patty's murder before the next startling revelation: "A witness has come forward, and police are seeking *this man*, whom they've called a person of interest in this case."

When the police sketch of the man appeared on the screen, I caught my breath. Although the drawing was a pencil sketch, it was quite detailed, and I recognized the face immediately: it was the same man who'd delivered the black roses to Tracey!

"Police are asking for help from the public to identify this man. If you know him or his whereabouts, call the Center City Police Department tip line," the announcer continued. "You may remain anonymous," he said, as the phone number for the tip line flashed on the screen.

My hands trembled as I fumbled for my phone. I couldn't speed dial Wes fast enough.

"Hi, gorgeous. I take it you watched the news," he said.

"I did, and I have some news for you. The police sketch shows the delivery guy, the same one who brought Tracey the black roses and showed up yesterday at Lisa's house with flowers."

"You're sure?"

"Positive. The sketch looks just like him."

"I don't like the sound of this at all," Wes muttered.

"I know. Did you ever have a chance to check with those flowers shops yesterday?" I knew that if Wes had contacted them, it had been on an unofficial basis, so he shouldn't have any qualms about telling me.

"I did, and I had no luck, but since you saw the flower delivery yesterday at Lisa's house, I can report a sighting of the guy to Walker, and he can follow up by showing the sketch around at the local florists. Maybe seeing the sketch will jog someone's memory."

"I guess that's not much help, considering we have no idea who he is or where he lives."

"It's a lead. In the meantime, there's a good chance somebody will recognize him and call in. I don't like to think there's a connection to Tracey, though. I assume she's at work?"

"Yes. I talked to her a little while ago. Liam called and wanted me to convey his apology to her, but he was apologizing for not taking 'no' for an answer when he persisted in asking her for dates, even after she was adamant about turning him down. He still maintains that he didn't have anything to do with sending Tracey the flowers."

"I may have to have another talk with Mr. Murphy."

"He's terrified that he could lose his job, Wes. He really sounded sincere. If you see him, do you think you could do it after work hours? If he's telling the truth, I'd hate for him to lose his job because of something he didn't do."

"All right. I'll still keep it unofficial, too. We have no proof that he's done anything wrong, only suspicion."

"Could you play it a little bit cool when you talk to Liam?" I'd seen Wes in his detective mode, and he came across as stern, to say the least. "I know it's asking a lot, but he might react better."

"I suppose." I could tell Wes wasn't crazy about my suggestion, so I didn't push it any further. "Could you let Tracey know that she should be extra cautious, especially when she leaves work?"

"Of course. I'll tell her right away."

"You be careful, too, sweetheart. We don't know what or who we're dealing with, and Liam's already called you today."

"I will."

"I'm going to ask Luke to have your gate guards be on the alert for the delivery guy and for Liam. I know the flower man didn't come through one of the Hawkeye Haven gates when he brought the roses to Tracey, but you never know. It's worth a shot. We're still on for dinner tonight, aren't we?"

"You bet! I'll see you later. I love you."

"I love you, too."

The more I thought about the mysterious delivery man, the more I wondered who the witness might be. I had a pretty good idea, so, after I called Tracey to let her know the news and caution her to take care, I phoned Amy and asked her if she'd heard from Marcie. When she told me that Marcie had contacted her about an hour ago, I suggested that I visit Amy to find out all the details, but she insisted on coming to my house, instead. I figured that she must have had something out in plain sight in her living room that she didn't want me to see. I suspected that maybe she was wrapping a wedding gift from the coy way she'd deflected my request.

If I could just concentrate on our wedding plans and

nothing else, I'd be happy, but I couldn't help thinking about the terrible events of the past week.

Amy lived across the street from Cynthia on the same street as Tracey, so she didn't have far to come, and she was soon knocking on my door. Bear raced to see who was visiting, and he sat up for Amy with his big paws curled under his chin.

"How cute!" Amy exclaimed as she petted Bear. "What an adorable boy you are, Bear."

Bear panted rapidly in excitement and danced around us as we walked into the den.

I could see little beads of perspiration on Amy's face.

"Did you walk over?"

"Yes. I tried to stay in the shade most of the way, but it's still really hot out there."

"How about some iced tea?"

"That sounds good. Thanks."

"I can run you home later, so you don't have to battle the heat again," I offered.

"Great! I'll take you up on the ride. I feel a bit wilted; that's for sure."

I handed her a tall glass of iced tea and offered her some sugar, which she turned down.

"That's good and strong," she said. "Just the way I like it. Aren't you going to have a glass?"

"For sure. Drinking something helps fend off the hunger pangs."

"Maybe you're going a little overboard on your diet, Laurel. We wouldn't want you to pass out at the wedding!"

"Oh, I'll be all right. It's not long now, and I'll make sure I have breakfast the day of the wedding."

"It's getting close now. I'm so happy for you and Wes."

"Thanks, Amy," I said with a smile. "Me, too!"

Bear wandered over and gently nuzzled my hand. "No more snacks right now, Bear," I said as I petted him, and he lay his head on my lap.

"Bear's going to miss you while you're on your honeymoon. Is he staying with Fran and Brian?"

"Yes, for a while. My parents will stay here until Tuesday, so Bear can stay home with them. After they leave, he's going to stay with Fran and Brian until we get back. He's been monitoring me pretty closely lately. I think he knows something's up."

"I bet he does. He's a smart boy."

Bear looked up and let out a brief "woof," as though he agreed with Amy completely. We both laughed.

"I'm dying to find out what Marcie said when she called you," I prompted Amy.

"Oh, right. I got so distracted that I almost forgot. First, she asked me the result of the vote. I was surprised that she didn't call me right after the meeting, but I imagine she probably guessed the outcome. Anyway, I really didn't want to talk to her because I figured she'd turn nasty again."

"How did she take the news?"

"Quietly, if you can believe it. I felt a little sorry for her, so I asked her if she was all right, and then the dam burst."

"What do you mean?"

"She told me she'd been arrested early this morning, but she was out on bail, and she used her last dime to hire Carla Lawson as her attorney."

"Carla Lawson's supposed to be the best criminal attorney in Center City," I said. "Her 'last dime' must have been thousands, probably some of the thousands she embezzled from FFF."

"It must be. So according to Marcie, Carla talked to the district attorney and, when she came back to

Marcie, she told her that he was ready to prosecute her case vigorously, and he wouldn't consider a plea deal unless she cooperated. Marcie said she freaked out because she didn't want to go to prison. I guess it was finally sinking in that it could easily happen."

"She must have been in denial."

"Marcie told Carla that she didn't have any more money, so she didn't have a way to offer restitution. Then she asked Carla if the district attorney would consider recommending no jail time, but only parole, if she provided them information in a high-profile murder case."

"You're kidding," I said, but even as I said it, I realized that she had to have been talking about Patty's case. "She's the witness!"

"That's right! She said that she saw Patty being attacked and thrown into the pool at that house you and Wes were going to look at Sunday. She claimed she was going to call for an ambulance, but you and Wes showed up first, so she slipped out the front door when Wes dived into the pool. She said she got a really good look at the guy, but he couldn't see her because the patio doors have sun-blocking window film on them."

"I believe it because when I saw the police sketch of the guy on the noon news earlier, it looked just like him."

"What? But you said you and Wes didn't see anyone else around when you pulled Patty out of the pool."

"We didn't, not then. But it's the same guy who came to the door during my shower Saturday. I don't think you saw him, but Bear barked up a storm when he came to the door."

"Oh, right. Well, that's scary. What was he doing at Tracey's house?"

"A delivery." I explained about the dead, black roses.

"I'm positive it's the same man. I have no idea what the connection might be between the delivery and his attack on Patty."

"Maybe there isn't one."

"Maybe. Did Marcie happen to say why she was inside the house?"

"She said she was staying there, that there'd been a mix-up about her rent payments, and Patty was trying to make it up to her by letting her stay there temporarily until she resolved the issue. Marcie confided that she thought Patty had kept the rent money herself."

"Wouldn't that be ironic? One embezzler gets scammed by another embezzler. It kind of makes my head spin."

"Now that Marcie's out on bail, I wonder where she'll stay."

"A motel for a while, I guess. Her parents wired her some money. I don't think she told them the whole story."

"Probably too embarrassed. I'm sure they thought she was doing a fantastic job at work."

"We all did until the embezzlement came to light. Hopefully, she can find another job and pay FFF back some of the money. Her attorney advised her that the district attorney would require a payment plan agreement as part of the plea bargain. I'm sure she'll agree because I think she'd do just about anything to stay out of jail."

"Nobody can deny that she's an expert at public relations. Maybe Roger can revive that job offer that he talked his son into making Marcie when we were trying to resolve this issue a few months ago."

"I guess it's a possibility. It could be a win-win for everybody. Why don't I check with him and find out what he thinks about the idea?"

"Sounds like a plan. It just irritates me that she could have accepted Roger's offer in the first place, and she could have made restitution to FFF and avoided a warrant being issued for her arrest. I guess some people just have to learn the hard way."

"Well, Marcie's certainly one of them. She's led us a merry chase; that's for sure. At least, she's finally come to her senses."

"Sort of. She should have reported what she saw to the police right away."

"But she didn't because she knew she'd be arrested."

"Not only that but she knew she shouldn't have been staying at that house. Patty had no right to let her do that. Lisa told me it wasn't available as a rental."

We both sighed, leaned back, and sipped our iced teas. Marcie's fifteen minutes of fame—or, infamy, in her case—would end with the disposition of her case by a judge after the district attorney made his sentencing recommendation.

"I do hope Roger can get Marcie a new job offer from his son," Amy said. "If she accepts, she'll have to move to California."

I nodded. Walker must have been satisfied that Marcie witnessed the crime, rather than committing it herself. Otherwise, she'd have been charged in Patty's death, rather than having been released on bail.

"On a lighter note, Laurel, would you mind if I took a peek at your wedding gown?" Amy asked. She hastened to add, "I would totally understand if you don't want anyone to see it until the wedding, though."

"Not at all! Wes is the only one banned from seeing it before the wedding, not that I really think it would bring bad luck, but I want him to be surprised. The gown doesn't really look like much draped over the hanger. How about if I try it on to show you right now?"

"Yes!" Amy practically squealed in excitement. With her penchant for romance, she found every part of wedding preparations enchanting.

"Let's go in the bedroom," I said, "and I'll model it for you. I haven't tried it on since I started my diet."

Bear followed us into the bedroom where Amy sat on the loveseat next to the bed, and Bear lay at her feet, awaiting my grand entrance. The master closet was huge, one of the features I loved about my house. I'd hung my wedding gown carefully on the highest rung with plenty of space on either side of it so that no other clothing touched it and it didn't touch the carpet on the floor. I quickly undressed and put on the smooth, light-as-air, one-piece undergarment that fit like a second skin. I would wear it on the Big Day so that no unsightly underwear lines would show through the revealing dress. I slipped into the dress and adjusted the waistline sash, tying it in a bow in the back.

Parading into the bedroom, I executed a little pirouette in front of Amy so that she could see the gown from every angle.

"Oh, Laurel! How stunning!" Amy exclaimed. "That's true Hollywood glamor, and your gown fits you like a glove. The fabric looks absolutely luscious, too!"

"It's silk charmeuse. I was lucky my silk supplier had just the right blue I wanted. Otherwise, I would have had to dye the silk. You really think it looks okay?"

"No, it doesn't look 'okay.' It looks fabulous!"

"I guess I'm a wee bit insecure about wearing a slinky, bias-cut gown because the cut is really unforgiving. That's the reason for my diet. I didn't think I could afford to gain an ounce."

"You look perfect, and so does your gown," Amy

assured me.

I gladly accepted her reassurance. Although the floor-length gown didn't reveal much bare skin at all— there were two small V-shaped cutouts, angling left and right, at the neckline in the back, the front neckline draped gracefully just below where a jewel neckline would lie, and the three-quarter-length tulip sleeves covered most of my arms—I felt almost as bare as if I were wearing a bikini.

"When you've got it, flaunt it," Amy said, "and you've definitely, got it!"

We both laughed. "It's just that the gown is so clingy. I'm a little nervous about wearing it."

"Well, don't be. Everybody's going to rave about it, especially the groom." Bear sat up and gave a quick "woof" of approval.

"Thanks, Amy, and thank you, too, Bear." I'd been thrilled with the gown when I made it, but lately I'd started feeling that perhaps it was too daring to wear to my wedding, but since Amy had terrific taste, and she'd given me her seal of approval, I resolved to put my insecurities aside and wear the dress proudly.

I returned to my closet dressing room and changed back into my loose cotton gauze top, tan cotton pants, and sandals. I carefully hung my wedding gown on its padded hanger, making sure it draped properly and wasn't touching other clothing.

"How about another glass of iced tea," I offered when I emerged.

"That sounds good, but after that, I'd better go. I have some chores to finish before I go to dance rehearsal later."

I handed Amy her iced tea and poured myself another one, too.

"Are you going to wear one of those cute little

birdcage veils?" Amy asked. "I saw the sample you made for your DIY Bridal Crafts class, and I thought it was very chic."

"Thanks. I was debating on whether I would wear a birdcage veil or a hair vine, but I decided the thirties' glamor look called for a flower in my hair instead, so I made one from the same fabric as the dress."

"Sounds lovely."

"I'll show you. Let me grab my hat box." I went back to the closet, found the little hat box I was looking for, and returned to the den, but when I opened the lid, I was in for a surprise.

"Oh, no! I can't believe it!"

Chapter 18

"What's the matter?"

"I cut out the fabric to make the flower, but I never made it! I must be losing it, Amy. I was sure I'd already made it. How could I have forgotten to sew the flower?" I felt truly perplexed because I'd been so sure that I'd completed it.

"Well, it's not as though you didn't have anything else on your mind. You can't blame yourself for being a bit distracted."

"Here I thought I had everything ready for Saturday. It's a good thing you mentioned it. Otherwise, I would have been scrambling to finish my flower right before the ceremony."

"How long will it take to make it?"

"About an hour. I'm sewing the same little faceted Swarovski crystal beads in the center of the flower that I used when I made the rose gold earrings I'm going to wear. I like to sew the crystals on individually. I think it looks so much nicer than gluing them on."

Amy beamed as she stood and gave me a hug.

"You're going to be a beautiful bride! Shall we go now so that we can both get to work?"

"Sure. I'll grab my keys." I rummaged around until I found my keys in the depths of my handbag. As Amy and I started walking down the hall toward the door to the garage, Bear whimpered softly. I detoured into the laundry room and picked up his collar and leash.

"Do you want to go for a little ride, Bear?"

He ran to me and didn't even wiggle as I put his collar on him and attached his leash. As soon as I started the car, I turned the fan on high and blasted the air conditioning. Then I adjusted the vent in the back seat so that Bear would be getting plenty of air. He panted all the way to Amy's house, anyway, even though I was shivering from the cold air.

"Thanks for the ride, Laurel. Oh, I meant to tell you. Cynthia and I will have your cake set up well before the ceremony Saturday. Don't worry about a thing. We'll coordinate with your mom and Tracey."

"Great! I really appreciate it."

"See you Saturday."

As long as I was out, I decided to make a quick trip to the bank. I'd made out a deposit slip for a few checks students had given me to purchase supplies for their projects and my monthly check for teaching classes at the Hawkeye Haven Community Center. My bank was about a mile down the road from Hawkeye Haven's front gate, so it took me only a few minutes to drive there. When I pulled into the drive-through lane to make my deposit, there were three vehicles ahead of me. Only one lane was open, and cars were moving at a slow pace, but I couldn't go inside because Bear was with me, and I'd never leave him in a hot car. I didn't ever leave him alone in the car in any case, anyway.

Finally, we made it to the front of the line, and I sent my deposit through a pneumatic tube to the teller. Bear pressed his nose to the back window and looked right at the teller, who waved to him. Bear knew all about the bank because, whenever we stopped there, he was rewarded with a treat in the shape of a dog bone. Of course, he didn't care about the shape, although I thought it was cute, but he did savor the treat. As soon as he heard the whir of the pneumatic tube he angled his nose over my shoulder, eagerly waiting for his snack. He wasn't disappointed. In fact, this particular teller must have thought he was cute because there were two treats alongside the receipt for my deposit and the cash I'd withdrawn. I handed one of the snacks to Bear, and he crunched it with relish. Even though I'd palmed the second treat, he must have smelled it because he was back in a few seconds and nuzzled my hand until I gave it to him.

Loud honking startled me, and I glanced back to see an impatient driver waving me on. Nobody had been behind me the entire time we'd waited in line, so I didn't realize that a car had pulled up while I was giving Bear his snacks. I hurriedly pulled out and went on my way.

As I approached Hawkeye Haven's front gate, I saw Luke standing outside. He was probably subbing for a few minutes while the guard on duty took a break. I swerved over from the residents' lane, into the visitors' lane, so that I could talk with him.

"Hi, Laurel. Hey, there, Bear."

"Hi, Luke. I was wondering whether Wes had called you about the picture of that guy the police are looking for."

"He sure did. I printed a couple copies and posted them at both guardhouses. Also, I flagged Liam Murphy's name in our computer system with a note to check with me before granting him entrance. I understand that it's possible that Murphy may have some connection to the wanted man."

"It's possible. At this point, nobody knows for sure. Wes wants to take every precaution, though."

"Well, I'm happy to cooperate. The guards have all been alerted, and we'll be on the lookout."

"That's good."

"I ordered an extra patrol past Tracey's house, too."

"Thanks, Luke. We appreciate your help."

I waved as he opened the gate and I drove through. Although the Hawkeye Haven Homeowners' Association could be a giant pain with its numerous rules and regulations, it provided some measure of security. The system wasn't foolproof, though. The delivery guy hadn't come through either gate when he got into Hawkeye Haven on the day of my shower.

At home, Bear jumped out of the back seat as soon as I opened the door for him. Immediately, he ran to his water bowl and lapped up all the water. I refilled it, and he drank some more before lying down on the cool tiles of the kitchen floor.

Reminding myself that I needed to make my flower so that I'd have a hair accessory to wear with my wedding gown, I went to my craft room to retrieve a sharp needle, waxed thread, scissors, and the Swarovski crystal beads I'd use to embellish the center of the flower. The hat box with my fabric was still sitting on the coffee table where I'd left it after I'd discovered that I'd never finished my project. I put my supplies on a tray and settled down on the sofa in the den. With the afternoon sun flooding the room, the light was better in the den this time of day than it was in my craft room.

I threaded my needle and began to work. Hand sewing worked better for this project than machine sewing, as I worked the smooth waxed thread in and out of the drapey charmeuse fabric. After I'd formed the flower and tied off my thread, I began sewing the crystal beads in the center. I sewed each one individually, rather than stringing several together at one time, so it took a while before I'd placed all the beads just where I wanted them and sewed them securely in place.

There was just one more step before I finished, and that was to add a hair clip to the back of the flower. I rummaged around my craft room until I finally remembered where I'd stored some alligator hair clips. One of these would secure the feather-light flower in my hair. I found a little piece of light blue felt, too. I cut out a small circle of felt, cut a tab in it, and sewed it to the back of the flower. Now I slid the alligator clip through the tab and positioned the silk flower in my hair. I moved it around, trying various positions until I decided that it looked best on my left side a few inches above my ear. Satisfied with my pretty blue flower, I placed it in the little hat box, nestling it in white tissue paper, and tucked it away on a shelf in my closet.

Working with my dress fabric reminded me that I'd told Liz I'd hem a square of Tracey's dress fabric and make some bias fabric strips to decorate the corsages and boutonnière, so, while Bear napped, I cut and hemmed them. Although I had enough of Tracey's dress fabric to make a large square that Liz could wrap around the flower stems in Tracey's bouquet, there wasn't enough left to make the bias strips, so I made them from the baby blue silk charmeuse fabric that I had left after I'd made my wedding gown.

As soon as I finished, I went next door to drop them off to Liz. Although Bear had begged to go with me, I knew Miss Muffet wouldn't appreciate a visit from my furry companion.

"Laurel, come in out of the heat," Liz urged.

Miss Muffet had been perched on top of her kitty climbing tree, but, as soon as she saw me, she jumped down and scampered off to hide. Miss Muffet is strictly a one-woman cat. She'd cuddle with Liz, but she wouldn't let anyone else near her.

"Sometimes I wish she weren't so antisocial," Liz

said with a sigh, as she watched Miss Muffet run away.

"She's not antisocial with you, Liz. She's happy, and that's what counts."

"You're right. What do we have here?" Liz asked, as she peeked in the box I'd handed her.

"It's the fabric to decorate Tracey's bouquet and the other flowers."

"Of course. I should have remembered because it's on my to-do list."

"Maybe I should have a list, too. I almost forgot to make the flower that I'm going to wear in my hair for the wedding, and here I thought I had everything covered."

"Come and sit down for a few minutes, Laurel," Liz urged. "I know you're organized, but it might make you feel better if we do just that."

For the next half hour, Liz and I poured over all the wedding plans, noting every detail in her little notebook. When we finished, she smiled at me.

"I can't think of another thing," Liz declared. "All you have to do is show up on Saturday!"

"Thanks, Liz. I feel better. For a while there, I thought I might be losing it. I'm starting to feel a bit nervous," I admitted.

"Perfectly understandable. Getting married is a big step in life. A few pre-wedding jitters are normal."

"I guess so. Well, I should head back. I didn't realize it was getting so late. I need to feed Bear before I get ready to go out to dinner with Wes."

I could feel myself tearing up as I waved good-bye to Liz, who'd been a good friend to me ever since I'd moved to Hawkeye Haven. I wasn't usually quite so emotional, but with my upcoming wedding, raw feelings surfaced every once in a while. I resolved to get a grip as I swiftly wiped a stray tear from my cheek.

I certainly didn't want Wes to have to deal with my blubbering all evening.

After I gave Bear his dinner, I let him outside. I figured he wouldn't stay long because it was so hot. Humidity levels hovered in the upper double digits, and the muggy weather made me feel wilted whenever I went outside. Bear didn't linger long, and I slid the patio door open for him as soon as he came back to the patio. He wasted no time in emptying his water bowl, which I refilled promptly.

Still panting, he followed me as I went into my closet and tried to decide what to wear to dinner tonight. I'd really have to watch my calorie count, but Wes had hinted that he'd take me to a special place, so I wanted to dress up a bit. Eventually, I settled on seafoam green floor-length silk palazzo pants and a matching drapey top that I'd made several months earlier but hadn't worn much. I had only a few minutes to put on some make-up before Wes was due to arrive. I was fumbling through my eye shadows looking for a hue to match my clothing when my phone sang out "Endless Love."

When I saw Was was calling, I hoped he hadn't been delayed.

"Hi, sweetie. I'm just about ready," I said cheerfully. I was determined not to let my earlier pensive mood interfere with our evening together.

"I just this second got out of a meeting with the mayor's committee on crime prevention at city hall. The captain called me in to sub for him at the last moment, and I've been here most of the afternoon. I hate to say this, but I think I should go back to the station and put in several hours to wrap up my paperwork if I want to be able to start my vacation Friday."

"Oh, no," I said, trying hard to keep my

disappointment to myself. "What if I pick us up something and bring it to your office? You still need to have dinner, and I promise I won't stay long."

"That would be great! I'm really sorry about this. I had no idea the captain was going to tap me to stand in for him at the meeting, but I couldn't turn him down."

"I know. Rank hath its privileges." I was lucky I didn't have a boss to tell me what to do anymore, but I'd had several in the years before I'd launched my DIY Diva business full-time, and I knew the pressures a supervisor could bring to bear on employees. "What sounds good? I can call in our order and pick it up on the way to the station."

"A steak dinner would be nice, but I'll settle for pizza."

"One pizza coming up. Do you want the works?"

"Sure. Why not live dangerously?" Wes chuckled. "Don't bother with any drinks. I can get some pop out of the machine in the break room."

"Okay. How about a salad, too?"

"Sure. I really am sorry about this!"

As soon as we ended our call, I phoned the Pizza Palace and put in our order. The clerk told me it would be ready in half an hour, so I had plenty of time to finish putting on my make-up. I considered changing into something more casual since we weren't going to the restaurant, after all, but I didn't especially want to change clothes again, so I decided against it. I bade Bear good-bye and told him Mommy would be back soon. If Wes were going to get any work done tonight, I'd have to keep my visit short.

When I arrived at the Pizza Palace, my order was ready and waiting for me at the check-out counter. I paid with cash and stuck a few dollars in the tip jar. I'd ordered one large pizza and two salads. Since I'd been saving calories for the now-canceled restaurant meal, I figured I could have one slice of pizza and a salad without any dressing. The Pizza Palace employees always put salad dressing in a little plastic container separate from the salad. I'd ordered dressing with mine so I could give extra dressing to Wes. When he'd told me he'd like a steak dinner, I figured he was hungry.

When I arrived at the station, the desk sergeant recognized me and waved me through to the back area, where Wes's office was located. His desk was piled with file folders, and he was frowning at his computer monitor when I tapped lightly on the door frame. In an instant, he was out of his seat and moving the files to a credenza in back of his desk to make room for our food. I set the pizza and bag with our salads down on his desk top, and he gave me a quick hug and kiss.

"We could go into the break room," Wes said, "but I'd rather stay here, if you don't mind."

"So would I," I agreed.

"I got us a couple cans of pop and some water. What's your pleasure?"

"I'll take the water," I said, knowing that Wes preferred regular, rather than diet, cola. Wes handed me a bottle of ice-cold water. "Thanks."

"Umm. That's good," Wes commented as he bit off a chunk of pizza. He finished his first slice in less than a minute and helped himself to another one. "I skipped lunch today. I was just about ready to go grab a sandwich when the captain told me I was going to be his representative at the meeting. Boring!" He drew out the word, made a face, and rolled his eyes as he said it. "Now I have to write a report on it, too. Ugh."

I smiled at his droll expression. Wes hated paperwork. He was taking his third slice of pizza when his cell phone buzzed.

"What now?" he grumbled, glancing at his phone. "A guy can't even eat in peace." He picked it up and punched the display. "Wesson."

Wes listened for a while before he frowned and blurted, "You want to do *what*?"

Chapter 19

From the one side of the conversation I could hear, I was able to discern that Wes was talking to the teacher who had sub-leased his apartment, and it sounded as though he wanted to move in pronto, rather than waiting until Sunday, the date they'd originally agreed on.

"That would put me in a bit of a bind," Wes told him, "but I guess, under the circumstances, we can work it out. I'll need to make some arrangements. Let me call you back in half an hour or so."

Wes looked up. "Great," he groused. "The poor guy has no place to go after tonight. The folks he's housesitting for just let him know that they're going to return early from their vacation. They'll be back in town tomorrow morning, and he can't stay at their house any longer after they get back. He's short on cash, so he wants to move into the apartment tomorrow. I kind of hate to turn him down. He said he won't get his first paycheck from the school district for a month, and, in the meantime, his payment for the housesitting job will be the only money he has to live on. The poor guy sounded desperate."

"We could move most of your clothes tonight, and then while you're working tomorrow morning, I could pack up the rest of the books."

"That'd work I guess, and I can stay at Denise's Thursday and Friday night. With the girls staying in California for summer school this month, she has plenty of room, even though my parents will be staying there, too. I better give her a call."

While Wes called his sister, I munched my one allotted piece of pizza. It tasted so good that I was sorely tempted to have another one, but I opened my salad, instead, silently congratulating myself for sticking to my self-imposed diet. I took the extra serving of salad dressing and put it next to Wes's salad.

"Okay. I'm all set. Let's forget about moving anything tonight, though. If I can just get several hours in on this paperwork, it'll be a load off my mind. If you could start packing the books tomorrow morning, I'll take an early lunch and bring a dolly over, so I can move them. I don't want you carrying heavy boxes of books down the stairs. I can get the clothes then, too."

"Sure. That's fine. Too bad your landlord doesn't allow dogs on the premises. Otherwise, I could take Bear with me for company."

"You may have company. I'm not sure what time Cole's going to show up, but it'll probably be sometime in the morning."

"So he's going to be moving in while you're moving out?"

"Yes, but since neither one of us has much to move, I don't think it'll be a problem."

"I guess not. I may put him to work packing books if he's not careful. I forget. What's his last name again?"

"Larkin. Cole Larkin. You remember what he looks like, right?"

"Shorter than me and kind of thin with sandy hair, I think."

"Yup. I'm sorry to dump this on you, especially now. I know your parents are coming in tomorrow."

"It'll work out all right. Tracey and I will leave for the airport at two, so I'll have plenty of time in the morning. I have the house all ready for them, and I've even done the grocery shopping."

"I'll text him that you'll be at the apartment, so he can move in tomorrow morning and get the key from you."

"Fine," I said, glad that I hadn't scheduled anything for Thursday morning. Wes had a lot of books, and I had a feeling he hadn't packed any more of them since the last time I'd been there, right after we found Patty in the pool. "Oh, what about your bookcases? We need to move those, too."

"I think that can wait until we get back from our honeymoon. I'm doing Cole a favor by letting him move in early, so I doubt that he'd object to living with a few bookcases for a couple of weeks."

"True."

After Wes texted Cole, whose immediate enthusiastic response indicated that he was relieved that Wes had agreed to the early move-in, Wes took another slice of pizza.

"Don't you want some more?" he asked.

"No. I'm good," I told him.

"You're still on your diet, aren't you?"

I nodded sheepishly as he took my hand and told me how gorgeous I looked.

"That outfit you're wearing is pretty, too," he commented. "I meant to say something earlier."

Before I had the chance to thank him for his compliments, a ruckus broke out in the hallway

"Hey! I told you that you can't go back there. Wait a minute!"

Liam burst into Wes's office, followed by the desk sergeant, who was reaching for his handcuffs.

"Wesson, I want to talk to you!" Liam yelled.

"Not till you calm down," Wes said coolly. "If you

want to have a conversation, you need to lower your voice and behave in a civilized manner. Otherwise, you're going to spend the night in a cell."

By this time, the sergeant had grabbed his arms and was holding him back. Fear flashed in Liam's eyes, and he seemed to grow smaller right before our eyes.

"All right," he croaked. "Can I please talk to you?"

"It's okay, sergeant. I'll keep an eye on him," Wes said, and the sergeant left. Wes stood up and motioned for me to take his seat behind the desk. He sat where I'd been sitting and asked Liam to take the only other chair in the room.

"Now, where's the fire, Murphy?" Wes asked, as the two faced off.

"You said you'd leave me alone if I didn't contact Tracey. Well, I haven't called her or texted her, but you haven't kept your word," Liam claimed.

Then Liam looked straight at me and said, "Neither has she."

"Now wait just a minute—" I said.

"You leave Laurel out of it. This is between you and me. What are you talking about?"

"You know what I'm talking about. You sicced that other cop on me, that Lieutenant Walker. If my boss hadn't been in a meeting this afternoon when he came to the hospital to see me, I wouldn't have a job right now."

"Lieutenant Walker's investigating a homicide, and your name's come up as a possible lead in the case. The police aren't obligated to work on your time schedule."

"My name's come up? You mean you brought it up, don't you?" Liam's face was turning red. I could see him clenching and unclenching his fists as he talked to Wes.

"I'm doing my job, Murphy."

"Well, I wish you'd let me do mine!" he said bitterly.

"I'm not stopping you."

"Oh, right. First, you accuse me of doing something I didn't do, and then you put Walker on my case. If he comes to my office again during work hours, I'll lose my job."

Wes's skeptical look sent Liam into another diatribe.

"I'm not kidding! I don't have a secure government job like you cops do. My boss is looking for any excuse to fire me, and you're giving him one!"

"Aren't you being a little overdramatic, Murphy? Why would he fire you because you answer a few questions? That doesn't even make any sense."

"I tell you he has it in for me. It doesn't need to make any sense, except to him. For the last time, I did *not* send Tracey those dead flowers on Saturday."

"You're claiming you didn't recognize the sketch Walker showed you of the man he's looking for?"

"I'm not *claiming* anything. I'm telling you the truth!"

"Well, let's leave it for now. The truth will come out eventually."

"Eventually may be too late to save my job. Can't you at least ask Walker to stay away from my office?"

"Walker doesn't report to me, but I'll pass along your concerns. That's the most I can do. Like I said, it's his case."

Liam snorted in frustration. "I guess I'll have to be satisfied with that. I wish I'd never come back to Center City, and I wish I'd never met your cousin!" he said, looking me in the eyes. "I mean it. This has been the worst year of my life." He jumped up and exited through the open door. At least, he didn't slam it on his way out.

Although I was shaken by the unexpected encounter,

Wes appeared unperturbed as he reached for his salad and dumped both containers of dressing on it.

"Do you believe him, Wes? I remember when we talked to Liam on Sunday, you said you couldn't get a good read on him."

"Something's going on with Mr. Murphy; that's for sure, but whether or not it has anything to do with Tracey, I don't know. Time will tell. I know that sounds trite, but it's generally the case." He shrugged. "We'll just have to wait and see. With our perp's picture plastered all over the news, I really think there's likely to be a break in the case very soon."

We finished our dinner, Wes polishing off the rest of the pizza in short order. Although it was cold by now, he didn't seem to mind. My soon-to-be husband wasn't a picky eater, a fact for which I was grateful, given my lack of cooking skills.

"I really hope you can take Friday off," I said. "Aren't your parents going to be here Friday morning?"

"Yes. Denise can pick them up if I have to work, but I don't plan on it. I should be able to finish this paperwork by midnight. Tomorrow, Timmons and I have a few interviews scheduled, but they're just routine, going over the same ground again. I don't expect we'll have breaks in any of our open cases. Anyway, even if we do, Timmons should be able to handle things here. Don't worry, sweetheart. We'll be off on our honeymoon before you know it, and I promise I won't talk shop."

"How's your dad feeling?" I asked. Wes's father had had a heart attack a few months back, and he'd been recuperating at home.

"He says he's fine, and I'm sure they wouldn't be flying in for our wedding if Mom thought he wasn't up to it. She's watching him like a hawk to make sure he follows his diet."

"Which he hates, of course."

"Of course, but he had quite a scare when he had his heart attack, so he's not giving Mom too much grief over his diet. He really misses fried chicken and pie. They've always been his favorites, and now he has to avoid them. Salt, too. I can remember, even when I was a kid, that he used to salt his food before he even tasted it. No more of that, I guess."

"How about golf? Is he able to play again yet?"

"Yup. He's back to his twice-a-week games with his buddies in Phoenix. He may want to play while they're visiting."

"Hawkeye Haven has a nice course from what Cynthia and Pete tell me."

"I thought it was private, just for the residents."

"No, you don't have to be a resident to play. The golf course itself is open to the public. We should mention it to him."

"I'll do that. He always used to play at the city course when they lived here, but the last few times they've visited, he complained that the course wasn't being kept up the way it should be."

"Does Jack play?"

"No. Dad used to play with some of his old partners when he visited, but he told me the last time he was here that one of them has moved to Florida, another one went back to work, and the last of their original foursome had a stroke, unfortunately, and can't play."

"We'll have to introduce your dad to Pete at the wedding. He can probably play an extra game or two. He usually golfs on Sundays, but I bet he'd be up for another game."

"Good idea. I'll be sure to tell him. You know, I think he's actually nervous about standing up for me.

He said he's never been a best man before. I told him all he needs to do, really, is just stand beside me and hand me the ring."

"I'm sure he'll handle it just fine."

"He will. He always comes through in a pinch. Mom insisted that he get a new suit for the occasion. He's so used to hanging out in shorts and a tee-shirt now that he wasn't too thrilled about it, but he bought it. Mom assured me she has it all ready to go in a garment bag."

"I wish Derek had been able to come, too."

"Yeah. Me, too. If he had, Dad wouldn't have to worry about any of this. Well, I guess Mom probably still would have insisted that he buy a new suit."

"Did you happen to mention to Derek the possibility of our visiting him in Baltimore this fall?"

"I did, and he suggested that the week before classes start would be the best time. I wrote down the dates, but I'm not sure I'll be able to take more time off then."

"But, Wes, you have tons of vacation time coming, and you hardly ever take any."

"Right. I have the time, but I don't have the *time*. We're always so swamped here. Remember I told you that the city froze hiring and promotions, so we're not going to be getting more help anytime soon."

"Well, maybe you could at least take a couple of days, and maybe Derek could take us sightseeing in Washington. I've never been there, and I'd love to see as much as we can squeeze in."

Wes laughed. "It sounds like you've made up your mind to go."

"I'd love to go, but not without my husband!"

"Okay. I'll see what I can do to make it happen. I may have to attend more of those boring meetings at city hall to butter up the captain."

"Poor sweetie."

"You'd know how poor if you'd been there with me today. The meeting was so boring I almost went to sleep."

Voices and footsteps in the hallway outside Wes's office interrupted our conversation. I turned toward the door just in time to see Wes's partner Sergeant Timmons burst into the office. He hesitated just a split second when he saw me before nodding politely. I knew he hadn't been expecting me to be there because I seldom visited Wes at the station.

"What is it, Timmons?" Wes always called his partner by his last name, and Timmons referred to Wes as "lieutenant" or sometimes "boss." Although they'd been partners only a few months, they worked well together, and I knew Wes was relieved not to have to work closely with Felicia Smith any longer.

"Just heard a report that Smith spotted the perp they've been looking for. She's chasing him down right now!"

Chapter 20

"The guy in the sketch who was on the noon news today?" I couldn't help myself, even though I realized Timmons was giving the news to Wes, not me. I was bursting with curiosity. Maybe now we'd find out if there was a connection between the mysterious flower delivery to Tracey and Patty's untimely demise.

Wes frowned. "Is Walker with her?"

"No," Timmons said. "She's alone. She called in for back-up a few minutes ago."

"She could get herself killed pulling a fool stunt like that."

From down the hall in the bullpen area, a large open office with several desks jammed together, we heard a shout.

Wes jumped up and disappeared. I assumed he'd gone to find out what had happened. Timmons followed him, and I was left alone in Wes's office. Even though I was dying to find out if Smith had arrested the delivery guy, I knew I shouldn't try to join the officers in the bullpen; I'd be out of place and unwelcome. I waited impatiently for Wes to return to his office. Finally, after about twenty minutes, he came back.

"Sorry to dash off like that," he said. "It looks like the guy got away. Word is he may be wounded. The area is being searched, but, so far, there's no trace."

"Where did she find him? I mean in which part of town, or can't you tell me."

"Channel 6 is already there, and I'm sure the other

television stations won't be far behind, so there's no reason not to tell you. It was on the outskirts of the warehouse district, south of downtown. According to what I heard, the perp ran off, into a residential neighborhood nearby. That's where they're searching for him now. They've even launched the helicopter, but he's had a head start. He could have been long gone before any other officers arrived to look for him. He fired a shot at Felicia, and she got off a round before he took off. She chased him, but he was too fast for her to catch up to him."

"I wonder how in the world she tracked him down in the first place."

"No idea, but she shouldn't have been out there alone," Wes said disapprovingly.

"I should probably get going, so you can start on your paperwork."

"Wait just a minute, sweetheart. I want to walk you to your car, but, first, let me get rid of this." Wes picked up the empty pizza box and plastic containers. "I'll be right back. There's a big recycle can in the break room."

After Wes left, I took a last swallow of water. I figured I might as well add my water bottle and Wes's pop cans to the recycle bin, too. I remembered where the break room was, down the hall in the opposite direction from the bullpen. In the break room, several automatic machines for the officers and civilian staff to buy drinks and snacks lined the far wall. A large table with several chairs sat in the middle of the spacious room. Along another wall was a kitchen counter with a sink. A giant coffee maker and a microwave oven sat on top of the counter, and there were cupboards above. The room was brightly illuminated by the overhead fluorescent lights. I remembered that the last time I'd been there, one of the lights had been buzzing as well as blinking on and off.

As I neared the door, I could tell that the light still hadn't been fixed. I heard the buzzing and saw the blinking light even before I went into the room.

Just as I was about to enter the room, I heard another noise. It sounded like a woman sobbing.

I stepped into the room and had the shock of my life.

Wes and Felicia were standing off to the side of the table, and Felicia had her arms wrapped around Wes, sobbing on his shoulder.

I dropped the cans I'd been holding, and they clattered to the floor, startling the pair. Wes jumped back, dragging the clinging Felicia along with him. He gingerly tried to disentangle himself from her grasp, but she clung on for dear life, shooting me a smug look as she clutched my fiancé.

Felicia had disliked me from the moment we first met nine months ago. It was the first time I'd met Wes, too. They had come to my house because I'd been in the crowd at a murder scene in Hawkeye Haven, and they were questioning everyone who'd been there. After the pair had left, I'd overheard Felicia teasing Wes about me because he'd told her that he appreciated a beautiful redhead.

I remembered exactly what she'd replied, too: "Beautiful? With that mop of red hair? Give me a break! And that dog of hers was disgusting, wiping his fur all over my new white pants."

Wes hadn't let his former partner's opinion of me influence him, though, and he'd asked me out on our first date a few days later. Felicia had never changed her opinion about me, but it wasn't until several months later that I finally learned the reason for her dislike when Felicia told Wes that she loved him. We were already engaged at the time, but that didn't stop her. Wes had requested a change in partners, and, luckily, his captain had approved the move.

From the way Felicia was hanging onto Wes, it appeared that she hadn't given up yet, even though our wedding was just a few days away.

Wes stepped back again and finally succeeded in wrenching himself out of her arms. He grabbed a wad of paper towels from the dispenser under the cupboards and handed them to her. Her face looked suspiciously dry to me as she patted it with a paper towel. Although her eyes looked red, it wasn't the red following a crying jag, but looked more like her contact lenses had slipped out of place. Her sob story had all been an act, but Wes didn't see it. He looked distressed and told her he'd have one of the uniformed officers drive her home as soon as she'd been debriefed.

"I'll take her home, lieutenant," a voice coming from behind me said.

I turned and saw Timmons. If he was willing to take charge of Felicia, it was all right with me.

"Shall we go?" I asked Wes pointedly.

He nodded and followed me, leaving Felicia and Timmons alone in the break room. We walked outside without saying a word. A young couple was entering the station as we were exiting, and it wasn't until we'd descended the steps to the sidewalk that led to the visitors' parking lot that we could really be alone.

I turned to Wes. Although it was dark by then, I could see him in the glow of the lights from the visitors' parking lot.

"Duane Harris Wesson! Whatever were you thinking?"

"I wasn't thinking. All I did was react. After I dumped the trash, I turned around, and Felicia grabbed me. I didn't even hear her come into the room."

"A likely story!" I said, putting my hands on my hips. Although I tried to keep the twinkle out of my eye and the smile from my lips, Wes caught on.

"You're teasing me!"

I hugged him as he leaned down for a kiss.

"Guilty," I said, "but I have to admit that when I came in and saw you two together, I was taken aback. You know, I don't think I ever picked up those cans I dropped."

"I thought you were mad at me."

"Wes, your body language spoke loud and clear. I know you didn't encourage her. If I'm mad at anyone, it's Felicia."

"She's had a tough day. She said the perp shot at her, and then she got a round off. She's sure she hit him. She was crying because nobody's ever taken a shot at her before, and she's never shot anyone, either."

"I know you don't see it, but Felicia's playing you"

"What do you mean? She was upset, and that's not like her."

"Wes, she wasn't really crying. She was making noises, but I didn't see any tears. Is your jacket damp?"

"Uh, no," Wes said as he moved his hand over the fabric, "but there's something on it." He held out his hand, and I could see the remnants of make-up there.

"It's make-up, probably foundation," I said. "The dry cleaners should be able to remove it, but be sure to tell them what it is." I couldn't help myself that my practical fashion side kicked in.

"So she faked the tears?"

"Yes. I'm not saying she wasn't bothered by being shot at or by shooting someone else. Anyone would be, but she wasn't nearly as upset as she made out. The crocodile tears were strictly for your benefit."

"But I don't get it. Why would she do that? She knows we're getting married in a few days. I've never done a thing to encourage her, and I try to avoid her when I'm at the station."

"She still has feelings for you, obviously."

"But I don't have feelings for her! I've never thought of her as anything other than a colleague. I wish she'd just leave me alone."

"You and me both," I agreed. Much as I disliked the fact that Wes's former partner still worked in the same building as he, there wasn't anything either one of us could do to change that situation. I sighed.

"Promise you're not mad at me?" Wes asked

"I promise."

"Then let's seal it with a kiss," Wes said, and we proceeded to do just that.

Chapter 21

It had been an eventful day, but it wasn't quite over yet. I'd forgotten to leave any lights on, and when I arrived home, I fumbled in the dark for the hallway switch, nearly tripping over Bear as he danced around me. As soon as I flipped the light switch, I could see that he was literally jumping up and down for joy, his hind legs on the floor and his front legs bouncing.

As I slowly made my way through the house to open the patio door for him, he continued his antics before obligingly running outside. I stood on the patio waiting for him, and he soon returned, trotted into the house, and went straight to his empty food bowl. Then he looked up at me with his big brown eyes, and cocked his head to the side. I could almost hear him saying "please, I want some more," like Oliver Twist in the Dickens novel. My lovable Lab was hardly a hungry orphan, though, but I couldn't resist his pleading eyes, so I gave him several baby carrots and ate a few myself.

While I checked my email on my phone, Bear settled down on his bed in the den. I'd neglected to check my email at all today, but since it consisted mainly of advertising from retailers I'd made online purchases from, I quickly scrolled through the list, deleting as I went.

I was almost done with this daily task when I heard the music of my ring tone's latest song. I'd switched "Endless Love" for "Always and Forever," although both were in keeping with my pre-wedding mood.

My upbeat feeling took a rapid downturn as soon as I saw who was calling. "Hello, Lisa."

"You were supposed to call me so I could show you my new listing at two this afternoon."

"I told you that Wes had to work."

"He could have taken an hour off. Now you have one last chance. I have an opening to show you the property on Friday at eleven."

"Isn't Patty's funeral on Friday?"'

"It's after the funeral," she snapped, "and, Laurel, if you and Wes can't look at this house Friday, I'm going to have to cut you loose."

"Let me save you the trouble, Lisa. I'm cutting *you* loose. We're not going to look at any more houses before the wedding, which I've already told you, but you're not listening. When we get back from our honeymoon, and when we're ready to look for a house again, we'll find another agent. Your services are no longer required."

Lisa snorted. "That's fine with me. I can't afford to waste my time with so-called clients who can't make up their minds. You two are nothing but tire kickers." With that, she abruptly hung up.

Although I was relieved that we wouldn't have to deal with Lisa's pushy tactics any longer, the unpleasant conversation left me feeling less than serene. I thought about calling or texting Wes to let him know, but then I decided it could wait until tomorrow. He'd be deep in his paperwork by now, and I didn't want to interrupt him. I wanted him to be able to take Friday off just as much as he did.

While Bear snoozed, I spent the rest of the evening watching television, waiting for the ten o'clock news to find out if there'd been any new developments related to the man Smith had shot. Although Channel 6 aired some video of the earlier police search for the man Smith had shot, the anchor reported exactly the same story I'd already heard at the police station. After showing the police drawing of the suspect again, the reporter asked viewers to notify police if they saw him or knew of his whereabouts.

That was the lead story, and I didn't wait to hear more before Bear and I headed to bed. I knew my eager Lab would be up early the next morning, and, true to form, he woke at five o'clock, ready to go for his daily walk, despite our having spent a restless night, due to noisy thunderstorms. Bear hated the crashing thunder, which was so loud I wouldn't have been able to sleep through it myself, even if he hadn't barked every time the thunder cracked.

With a yawn, I rolled out of bed, and opened the patio door in the bedroom. We hadn't heard any thunder or seen any flashes of lightning for a couple of hours, so I hoped the storms had all passed by. When I went outside with Bear, I could see that the sky had cleared, so as soon as he came back inside, I dressed in jeans, a long-sleeved cotton top, and slip-on canvas walking shoes. My week-old bruises had turned color from purple to an ugly green hue, and I still wanted to hide them as much as possible, although it was doubtful that any other dog walkers I might encounter would take much notice or care, even if they did notice them.

Following our usual route, we quick-stepped for a few blocks and then settled down to a more leisurely pace for the rest of our walk. I waved to a few neighbors along the way, but we didn't see any other dog walkers. Maybe they were sleeping in after the night of noisy thunderstorms.

Over a cup of black coffee, I watched the early morning news, but the story about the suspect in Patty's death hadn't changed since the ten o'clock news the night before. I waited a while before calling Wes. He'd had a late night at the station, and he didn't normally rise as early as Bear and I did. He beat me to it, though. When I heard the strains of Heatwave's "Always and Forever," I knew it had to be Wes calling. Nobody else ever called me before eight.

"Good morning, sweetheart," Wes said cheerfully. "I finished every bit of paperwork, so I'll be free as a bird after work today, and, for once, I'm actually going to knock off at five o'clock."

"That sounds good. What time do you think Cole's going to show up at your apartment? I think I should be able to pack up the books in a couple of hours, so I thought I'd go over there around nine."

"Perfect. I'll take an early lunch and be there with the dolly around eleven. Since we're not moving the bookcases until after our honeymoon, do you want to stack the boxes in your office or maybe the garage?"

"It would probably be better to put them in the office. That's where they'll end up, anyway once we have the bookcases in place. There's no need to move them twice."

"All right. I hope you can squeeze some space in the master closet for my clothes."

"No problem. I've re-arranged my clothes, so you'll have plenty of space—well, adequate space—or maybe I should say a small space."

"Very funny. I suppose I'll manage."

"Seriously, I measured exactly how much room your clothes are taking up in your closet in the apartment and multiplied it by two. You should have plenty of room, but, if not, I can move some of my things to the closet in my craft room."

"I can tell you're way more organized that I am. In

my defense, I didn't realize Cole would need to move in early. I figured I'd have the whole day Friday to move stuff and pack for our trip."

"We'll be one step ahead then, since we'll have most of the move finished today, and you can pack on Friday."

"Okay. I'll see you in a few hours at the apartment. If I can leave the office for my lunch break earlier than eleven, I will, but the captain has a meeting scheduled for nine this morning, so you never know. Remember, don't lift any of those boxes of books. They're going to be really heavy once you pack them."

"Yes, sir! If I need to have them moved, maybe Cole can help me."

"I'm sure he wouldn't mind. I'll see you later. I love you, sweetheart."

"I love you, too."

Only two more days until our wedding! A year ago I hadn't even known Wes, let alone entertained any thoughts about marrying again. In fact, before I'd met Wes, I'd had only a handful of dates in the years since I'd become a widow. My life had certainly taken an unexpected turn.

Before I went to Wes's apartment, I needed to make sure my house was ship-shape for my parents' arrival. I quickly picked up odds and ends, made my bed, started the dishwasher, and gave the guest bathroom a final inspection. I straightened the towels, topped off the soap dispensers, and placed a fragrant dried floral arrangement on top of the vanity.

Since I figured I might not have much time to change clothes before Tracey picked me up, I quickly showered and put on a vivid green maxi dress. I had a loose, long-sleeved, drapey jacket that I'd made to match the dress, so I could cover my arms before Tracey and I met our parents at the Des Moines airport.

Bidding good-bye to Bear, who'd sensed something was up, I slipped out the door, distracting him by dropping one of the peanut butter treats he loved into his dish.

On the way to Wes's apartment, I couldn't help remembering that during the night, sometime between thunderstorms, I'd awakened, feeling sure I knew the key to the puzzling connection between the delivery of the dead roses to Tracey and Patty's death, but now, somehow, the connection escaped me. I wondered if I'd dreamed it, although I knew I'd felt sure about my insight at the time. Turning it over in my mind didn't help. Maybe if I didn't think about it for a while and concentrated on the work at hand, I'd remember.

When I arrived at Wes's apartment, there was no sign of Cole yet, so I unfolded one of the sturdy packing boxes, set it on the kitchen table, and got to work, putting books into it. It occurred to me that Wes would probably need to do some laundry before he packed for our trip, so I checked his hamper for the casual shirts he'd need for the trip and started a load of laundry. As I closed the lid of the washing machine, which was stacked under the dryer in an alcove next to the kitchen, the door buzzer sounded, signaling that someone wanted to come into the building.

"Cole?" I asked after I pushed the intercom button.

"Yeah. It's me. Could you please buzz me in?"

"Sure," I replied.

I opened the door in anticipation of Cole's arrival. Wes lived on the third floor, and although the apartment building had an elevator, it was at the other end of the hallway and slow, to boot, so Wes always took the stairs. When Cole showed up at the door, I could tell he'd done the same since he was panting from the two-flight trip up the stairs. He was half hidden behind a large box as he staggered into the living room. The flimsy box burst as he set it on the coffee table, but, luckily, it was filled with notebooks and other school supplies, and there was nothing fragile to break.

"Oh, rats," Cole said, gathering up the supplies and stacking them neatly on the coffee table. "Sorry about that," he muttered. "I'll take this box back down to the dumpster."

"Umm." I wasn't paying too much attention to what Cole said because I'd just remembered my insight from the night before, and it was a lulu. I needed to tell Wes, even though he'd probably think I was crazy, but when I glanced at the kitchen clock to check the time, I could see that he'd still be in his meeting. I hesitated, considering perhaps I should wait until he arrived to tell him my theory, but then I decided if there were any way to talk to him sooner, I should do it. I called the station and left an urgent message for him to call me as soon as the meeting broke up. After I stressed the importance of my message to the clerk who took it, she promised to relay it to Wes in person as soon as possible, but she said she would have to wait until the meeting wrapped up. There wasn't much else I could do. I'd just have to wait until Wes called.

"Laurel?"

"I'm sorry. I was distracted for a minute. Did you say something?"

"Yes. I wanted to let you know that a guy I worked with on a day job is here to help me move my stuff, although he's really not much help because he hurt his arm. Anyway, I told him if he helped me, he could stay here with me for a couple of days."

"What?"

"Just for a few days."

"Well, I don't know. You'll have to check with Wes." I didn't think a roommate was part of the agreement Wes had made with Cole. In fact, I was pretty sure that Wes had specified that Cole was to be the sole occupant of the apartment until the sub-lease expired. "He should be here later."

"Okay," he shrugged. "I'll do that." Cole didn't seem to care one way or another whether Wes approved or not. I surmised that maybe the young teacher was hoping that Wes wouldn't allow the man to stay, that he regretted asking him to help, since apparently he wasn't able to help much because of his arm.

Taking the crumped box with him, Cole left, telling me he'd be back in a minute.

While I carefully packed more books, I worried about how Wes would react when I told him my theory and whether or not he'd even consider it plausible. Right or wrong, I knew he wouldn't be happy about what I had to say.

The raucous buzzer sounded again.

"Sorry, Laurel. I'm going to find something to prop this door open with so I won't have to keep ringing the buzzer to come in."

"Oh, I forgot to give you your key. You can open it with that." I pressed the button to open the downstairs door.

"Okay, thanks. In the meantime, I'll wedge a stick in it. We'll be right up with another load."

This time when I opened the door for Cole, he carried two large trash bags. I stood back while he jockeyed them through the doorway. Another man followed him, dangling his right arm at his side, his left arm wrapped around a small box. He had his head down so I didn't recognize him at first, but as soon as the skinny, long-haired young man looked up and saw me, we locked eyes, and I could tell he knew I'd recognized him.

He was the same man who'd delivered dead black roses to Tracey, the same man who'd also presented flowers to Megan, the same man whose face had been plastered all over the local news!

Patty's killer stared at me with his steely gray eyes.

Chapter 22

Before I had a chance to react, he dropped the box he was carrying and shoved Cole aside with his left arm, kicking the apartment door shut with his foot in a swift movement.

"Hey, man! What do you think you're doing?" Cole protested, tripping over one of the trash bags he'd dropped, as he struggled to keep his balance.

"Shut up!"

"Now, look, Austin. I was trying to do you a favor by letting you room here with me a couple of days, but if that's the way you're going to act, you can't stay here. I think you'd better go now."

"I'm not going anywhere, and neither is she," Austin said. "Sit down over there on the couch—both of you."

"I will not," Cole said, advancing toward Austin. "You need to leave—now!"

"Get back!" Austin warned, pulling a switchblade from his pocket. In a flash, he switched open the deadly knife and waved it menacingly at Cole, who instinctively jumped back. This time, he did trip over the trash bag he'd dropped and went sprawling onto the floor.

Cole looked up in confusion.

"I said get on the couch. You, too, lady."

I slowly inched my way to the sofa and sat down, while Cole rose and backed up until he'd reached the sofa and plopped down.

"If you want money, you're barking up the wrong

tree. You know I don't have any," Cole told Austin. "I haven't cashed my housesitting check yet."

"It's not about money, Cole," I said, trying to keep my voice steady. "Austin's a wanted man."

"Yeah. I figured you knew that," Austin snarled. "I could tell when you saw me."

"Wanted for what?" Cole asked.

"He killed a woman," I said.

"That's a lie!" Austin protested. "I didn't do it."

"There's a witness who says you did," I said. "If you didn't do it, why don't you turn yourself in, and tell your story to the police?"

"A witness? No, there can't be. There wasn't anybody around—" he paused. When he stopped talking, mid-sentence, I was sure that he'd just realized he'd just admitted to attacking Patty. He wouldn't have been able to see Marcie from her vantage point inside the house, especially since she'd been standing behind a window that had sun-blocking film on it.

The color drained from Cole's face as he grasped the severity of our predicament.

"Uh, Austin, why don't you go ahead and leave," Cole suggested. "We promise we won't say anything."

"Yeah. Right. Her boyfriend's a cop! No way she's not going to rat me out to him."

"Well, okay, but you can be long gone by then," Cole told him.

Austin's eyes darted back and forth between Cole and me. For a minute, he actually looked as though he might be considering leaving us there while he made his escape.

"No can do. Where would I go? I won't have any cash until Michael pays us tomorrow."

The instant he mentioned Michael's name, another

piece of the puzzle fell into place, and I just had to ask him if he meant Michael Stanley.

"That's where I met him," Cole said bitterly, nodding toward Austin. "We both worked for Michael whenever he had a big landscaping job."

"I might have some money in my purse," I volunteered. Anything to get Austin to leave. I'd withdrawn some cash when I deposited my checks the day before, but I couldn't remember which purse I'd taken with me or whether I'd even left the money in the purse. "My handbag's on the table over there," I told Austin.

"You get it," he commanded, wincing and shaking his right arm. He didn't put the knife down, though, and he motioned with it.

I went to the kitchen table and retrieved my handbag.

"Get back here," he said.

I returned to the sofa, sat down, and started to open the purse.

"Oh, no, you don't. Dump it out there on the coffee table. Who knows what you have buried in that thing? You could have a gun for all I know."

I did as he instructed. Although there were plenty of other items in my handbag, a gun wasn't one of them. Looking at the pile of stuff that my purse had held reminded me of the game we'd played at my bridal shower. Now I wondered if I'd get the chance to become a bride.

Suddenly, the music of Heatwave's "Always and Forever" began playing. I itched to pick up my phone, which had been inside my purse and now lay in front of me on the coffee table. I reached for it before Austin swiped it away from me, and it clattered to the floor.

"Don't touch that phone," Austin said, kicking it across the room. "Where's the money?"

"I'll check," I said. "I don't remember how much I had in this purse." I reached into my wallet and pulled out a twenty. I opened it wider. The twenty was the only bill there. "Here," I said, offering it to Austin. "That's all I have with me."

"How far do you think I'll get on twenty dollars?" he asked, although he managed to grab the bill, despite his injured arm, and stuff it in the front pocket of his jeans.

Desperately, I tried to think of the best strategy to encourage Austin to leave the apartment. I could tell Austin that I was expecting Wes to come over, but then he might try to ambush him or hold us hostage. If only there were some way I could warn Wes, but, since I'd been separated from my phone, there wasn't anything I could do.

Obviously, Austin didn't have much of a plan. From what he'd said, I gathered that he was waiting for his payday. Cole had told me that Austin planned to stay with him for "a couple of days," and then later he mentioned "just a few days." To me, the time frame sounded open-ended. If I didn't miss my guess, Austin probably would have managed to persuade Cole to let him stay longer. Even with his pay in hand, it was unlikely that he could stretch it too far. I doubted that he could afford to leave town, but if he did stay in Center City, he'd have to lay low because the police were looking for him. Then there was his wound to consider. I suspected he hadn't had any medical care for it at all. It could easily become infected, and then he'd be in even a worse pickle than he was now. The whole scenario added up to desperation, and Austin was certainly desperate enough to pull something even more foolish, something that could get Cole and me seriously harmed or killed.

Maybe I could distract Austin by talking to him. I

hoped the phone call that Austin had prevented me from taking had been from Wes and that, when he couldn't reach me, he'd come to his apartment to check on me right away, rather than waiting until his lunch break. The problem was that the call could have been from anybody. Wes could still be in his morning meeting, and it could last longer than he'd anticipated.

Together, Cole and I might be able to overpower Austin, but we had no way of communicating with each other to form a plan, since Austin was right there in front of us, wielding his knife, and he could hear every word we said.

Without taking his eyes off us and still flashing his switchblade, Austin ground his teeth as he eased into a chair facing the sofa. I didn't know whether Smith's bullet was still in his arm or if it had passed through.

"You should get that arm looked at by a doctor," I said. "It's bleeding."

All three of us looked at his shirtsleeve, where a small red patch slowly expanded.

"Don't be a fool, Austin," Cole said. "If you turn yourself in, you'll get medical care."

"I'm not turning myself in. Are you crazy?"

I didn't want Austin to become even more agitated, so I thought I'd try to distract him. "Would you like something to drink? There's some pop in the refrigerator." There was also some beer in the refrigerator, but I wanted to avoid giving any to Austin. "Or I could make coffee."

Austin eyed me suspiciously.

"You can see the refrigerator from here," I told him. Then I realized that he'd have a problem holding the can and the knife at the same time, even if he accepted my offer. "I can get you a straw."

"Okay, but no funny business. Don't make any

sudden moves."

"I won't. You can see everything right from where you're sitting." As though he were a young child, I explained: "I'll just open the fridge, get a can of pop, and set it on the counter. The straws are in the cabinet next to the refrigerator. After I pop the top, I'll put the straw in the can and bring it to you."

"And I'll be right behind you the whole time. You're not going to have the chance to pull a gun or a knife on me," he declared. "And you," he said, looking at Cole, "don't move a muscle while I'm with her, or I'll slit her throat."

Hearing his threat, I regretted ever having suggested that I bring him a drink. I drew my breath in sharply and then took a few deep breaths to steady myself before I slowly rose and made my way into the kitchen.

Austin held the knife close to me as I opened the refrigerator a few inches so that he wouldn't spot the beer, reached inside, and pulled out a can of cola. I carefully set it on the counter, located the straws in the cabinet above, peeled off the protective paper, popped the top of the can, and put the straw into it. We went back to the living room, and after Austin sat down, I set the can on the wide arm of his chair. Still brandishing his knife and keeping his eye on us, he leaned over and drank through the straw.

The entire maneuver had bought us a little time, but not much. If I could only engage him in talking about something that would take his mind off his crime and our current situation, maybe I could stall him even longer.

Cole glared at Austin and looked as though he were about to say something. Angry as Cole looked, I was afraid that he might say something to set Austin off, so I jumped in.

"Austin, are you from around here?" I asked. "Did you go to high school in Center City?"

"What's it to you?"

"Oh, nothing. I just wondered," I said, trying to sound nonchalant, although I felt anything but. "I'm from Seattle myself. I've lived here almost six years now, but I'm still not used to the cold winters and the hot summers. The weather in Seattle may be rainier, but the climate is much milder." I knew I was starting to babble, but maybe it was having some effect. It almost looked as though Austin's eyes were beginning to droop. If he fell asleep, he might drop the knife, and Cole and I could probably rush him before he realized what was happening, even though the coffee table stood in our way.

As Austin dipped his head, never taking his eyes off us, to take another sip of cola, the music from my phone started playing again. Agitated, Austin jumped up. Moving swiftly, he strode to the phone lying in a corner where he'd kicked it earlier. He raised his foot and began stomping on it with the heel of his work boot. As I stared at my smashed phone, my heart sank. Was Wes trying to get in touch with me or was it just some telemarketer? Austin looked down at the rubble that had once been my phone and smirked.

In that split-second while he looked away from us, Cole seized the opportunity to throw one of the sofa cushions at him. I'm sure he'd hoped to knock the knife out of Austin's hand, but his pitch went wide, missing its mark.

I gasped as Austin rushed to Cole and held the knife at his throat.

"Please don't hurt him," I begged.

"He tried to hurt me!"

"No, he didn't, Austin. He only wants for you not to

hurt *us*. Don't you get it? You're scaring us. Look, I know you're scared, too."

"I am not," he protested.

I held up my hands. "Okay." Talking to him was like trying to reason with a petulant child. "But Cole is your friend. Didn't he offer to let you stay with him?"

"Yeah." He stood back, and Cole edged away from him.

"Well, then, you don't really want to harm him, do you?"

"I guess not."

Wes's home phone in the kitchen started ringing. Cole looked at me angrily, as though I'd made it happen.

"That's probably my fiancé calling. If I don't answer, he'll know something's wrong," I said.

"You're lying!"

I shrugged. "Wait and see."

"Okay. Answer it, but you better be careful what you say."

Managing to follow me while still keeping an eye on Cole, Austin flashed his knife.

"Turn it on speaker," he hissed.

"Hello."

"Good morning. This is Zena from Center City Communications, and I want to tell you about a great deal on satellite television. It's a limited time offer—"

Chapter 23

"Your fiancé, huh? Surprise!" Austin said harshly as I hung up the phone. "Now, get back in the other room."

Dejected as I was, I knew Wes would call, and, eventually, if he couldn't reach me, he would come back to the apartment. Would he show up in time? Austin seemed increasingly agitated. He jumped at every little sound we heard. I was afraid his nerves would get the better of him, and he'd lash out.

After Cole's attempt to knock the knife out of Austin's hand by pitching the pillow at him, I thought he'd given up on the idea of subduing Austin, but I was wrong.

As we walked back from the kitchen, Austin circled around the sofa, and Cole extended his foot just as Austin went by him. It did the trick. Austin fell to the floor, landing on his injured arm. Groaning, he tried to get up, but Cole jumped on him, pushing his arm down in an attempt to force the knife from his hand. Unbelievably, Austin held onto the switchblade, though. He rolled to the side, and Cole tumbled to the floor next to him. Now that he was able to reach Cole, Austin swiped wildly at him with the blade and finally connected, stabbing him in the side.

Grabbing his side, Cole yelped in pain. He staggered to his feet and collapsed on the sofa.

Suddenly, the apartment door flew open. My heart sank when Felicia Smith entered, her gun drawn. If I didn't miss my guess, she was not the solution to our troubles, but just the opposite.

"Well, well, what have we here?" she muttered. "Who are you?" This question was directed at Cole. She knew who I was, and I was certain she was well acquainted with Austin, too.

Still holding his side, Cole looked up at her. "I'm Cole Larkin. Who are you?"

Felicia wore street clothes, so there was no reason that Cole should have been able to identify her as a police officer.

"Never mind who I am," she told him. "So you're Wes's tenant?"

"You know Wes? Help us! This guy just stabbed me. Call an ambulance!"

Without looking behind her, Smith nudged the apartment door closed with her hip.

The sunburned skin on her face had started to peel, and she'd tried to cover it with make-up, which had formed little clumps all over her face. Odd that I hadn't noticed that the night before, when she held Wes in her clutches. She wore the same style of short, shapeless dress that she'd been wearing Sunday when she and Walker had appeared to take charge of the investigation into Patty's drowning at 2132 Maquoketa, only this dress was shorter than the other one and even baggier. To top it off, the chartreuse green color of the dress couldn't have been more unflattering. The strap of an ugly white cross-body bag was slung over her right shoulder, and the bag rested against her left hip, creating an unsightly bump in just the wrong place. Although I took her appearance in automatically, I had no time to dwell on it because I knew I was in for the fight of my life.

Trying to hide, Austin crouched behind the sofa, but

Smith had spotted him the minute she came in.

"Get out from behind that sofa, Austin," Smith said.

"No. You'll shoot me again."

"I'll shoot you right this second if you don't stand up."

Austin slowly rose, still clutching the open switchblade in his hand.

"Drop the knife," she ordered. I heard it fall to the floor. "Get over there," she told him, gesturing with her gun.

Austin complied. Cowering, he moved back to the chair where he'd sat earlier.

"What's going on?" Cole asked me. "Who is she?"

"She's a cop, a detective with the Center City Police Department," I said.

"So you're here to arrest Austin," Cole said to Smith. "You've got him. Can't you please call for an ambulance now? He stabbed me!"

"Good idea. Please call an ambulance for Cole," I said, although I knew that wasn't her intention.

"Oh, I'll be calling for an ambulance all right, but not yet."

"What are you waiting for?" Cole asked. "I'm in pain here. I need help."

"I'm afraid Sergeant Smith finds herself in a bit of a dilemma," I said. Although my voice sounded strong, I felt sick with fear. I knew she couldn't afford to merely arrest Austin, because he could testify that he'd been doing her dirty work. Everything she'd said and done since she'd appeared at Wes's front door confirmed my suspicion that Smith had been behind the attack on Patty, the delivery of the bouquet of dead roses to Tracey, and the incident in the parking lot where Wes and I had almost been run down. When she found out Marcie had been a witness to Patty's drowning, she knew she'd have to get her hired gun out of the way, but her shot had left him wounded, rather than dead. He was still a loose end, and I had no doubt she intended to take care of that loose end right away.

Cole had the misfortune of being the innocent bystander in the room. As for me, Smith's dislike of me seemed to have grown exponentially to some kind of an obsessive mania. She hated me enough to want me dead.

"What do you mean?" Confused, Cole looked back and forth between Smith and me.

"Shut up!" Smith interjected as she cannily scanned the living room. Using her left hand, she fumbled with the clasp of her cross-body bag, reached inside, and withdrew a small hand gun. "Here's how it's going to go down: I got a tip that my suspect was here. He'd already shot this guy," she said, nodding toward Cole, "and he tried to shoot me. Too bad Laurel had to get caught in the crossfire. After that, I shot him. End of story."

"That's not going to fly," I told her, stalling for time. "What tip? You know the department will call in the state police if an officer is involved in a shooting, and they'll investigate thoroughly. Where's the evidence that you ever got a tip?"

"Okay. So I spotted him on the street and tailed him here. There's no way they can prove that I didn't."

"And he just happened to end up in your former partner's apartment? Sounds like quite a coincidence to me. I doubt that they'll buy it."

"How would you know, Miss Smarty Pants? You think you're such a great detective just because you solved a couple of crimes. Wes and I have solved more than a hundred together."

"So you're going to get rid of me, thinking you two

can be together again. That's never going to happen. He doesn't love you."

Fury transformed Smith's face, and I instantly regretted reminding her that Wes didn't have feelings for her.

"Enough! You all stand right where I tell you, or I'll shoot you right this second," she snarled.

"If you really expect us to stand here and do nothing while you figure out the right angle to shoot from, you can think again." I looked at Cole and Austin. Even though they were both wounded, they weren't entirely out of commission. "There are three of us and only one of her," I said to them. "We can stand here like sheep and let her shoot us, or we can try to take her out together."

"But she has the gun," Austin protested.

"And you, of all people, should know she won't hesitate to use it," I said. "We may get hurt or killed. That's the chance we'll have to take. If we don't do something now, we'll definitely be killed." My speech may have sounded brave, but I felt far from it.

Smith looked uneasy as she repeated her command for us to stand up.

"If you shoot us where we're sitting, you won't be able to stage the crime scene," I told her.

"I've had it with you, once and for all, Laurel McMillan. You're going to go first."

Pointing her gun straight at me, Smith took a step forward. She didn't see Cole surreptitiously grab one of the notebooks he'd stacked on the coffee table earlier. This time, his aim was true, and the notebook knocked her service revolver out of her hand. I followed by grabbing the only thing that was within my reach. Throwing a pillow at her didn't cause any damage, but it added to the confusion. Austin struck the last blow with a heavy tape dispenser that had been among Cole's school supplies. It hit Smith in the side of the head and sent her reeling, although she didn't lose her balance.

The three of us jumped up, but, even though Cole had succeeded in knocking her service revolver out of her right hand, she still held the other gun in her left hand. She swiftly transferred it to her right hand and waved it at us as we advanced toward her.

Behind Smith, the door opened, and, the instant I saw Wes there, I shouted, "Help!"

Smith turned, and when she saw Wes, she deflated like a hot-air balloon low on helium.

"Give me the gun, Felicia," he said, holding out his hand.

Chapter 24

Smith meekly handed over her gun and burst into tears—real tears, this time. Then she tried to embrace Wes, but he fended her off. Instead of nestling in Wes's arms, she ended up in handcuffs.

Austin tried to make a run for it, but he couldn't get past Wes, and since there was only one way out of the apartment, he was trapped. Wes trained his Glock on Austin and made him lie, face down, on the floor until the uniformed officers Wes had called for back-up arrived. In the meantime, Wes read the two miscreants their rights.

As soon as Smith had been escorted out by two burly officers, Austin, accompanied by two other officers, was taken by ambulance to St. Anne's. Cole gave us a weak grin and a thumbs-up as paramedics strapped him to a gurney for transport in the second ambulance.

Wes closed the door after Cole's departure, and we fell into each other's arms. Now that the excitement was over, I couldn't seem to stop shaking.

"I got your message, sweetheart, and I knew, when you didn't answer the phone, something was wrong."

"So that *was* you calling on my cell phone," I said. "I wasn't sure." I pointed ruefully to my smashed phone. "Austin wouldn't let me answer it."

"I can see that," Wes said wryly. "We'll get you another one right away. You know, it's a good thing you clued me in about Smith's behavior last night. Otherwise, I might not have reacted as quickly as I did when I came in. I heard the commotion as I was coming down the hall. As soon as I saw she was pointing the gun at you, the big picture came to me in a flash. It's still hard to believe that the partner I worked with for five years could be capable of plotting murder. I suspect she'll deny everything."

As it turned out, Wes was absolutely right. Smith denied knowing Austin prior to her shooting him as well as any involvement in Patty's murder or the parking lot attack on Wes and me.

I was right, too. Because a Center City police officer had been charged with a crime, Wes's captain called in the Iowa Division of Criminal Investigation. They uncovered evidence that Austin had once served as an unofficial snitch for Smith, when she'd worked in vice investigations. Austin claimed she masterminded his attack on Wes and me in the parking lot, for which he'd "borrowed" Michael's truck. Michael hadn't known anything about it. Austin's task was to "get rid" of me, although Smith hadn't told him exactly how to accomplish it.

I'd been the target of all three bizarre incidents all along, only I'd been so wrapped up thinking about our upcoming wedding that I hadn't figured it out until almost too late. When I'd finally had a flash of insight, I'd realized that I was the link all along.

I'd been puzzled by the fact that, although Austin had recognized me when I'd confronted him outside of Lisa's house, he'd attacked Patty because he'd mistaken her for me. That mystery was solved when we later learned that not only was Austin extremely near-sighted, but he was also color blind. Seeing shades of red as gray, he was unable to distinguish hues. My natural auburn red hair didn't look anything like the shade of Patty's dyed burgundy red hair, but Austin couldn't tell the difference. He knew he was supposed to target the redhead, so he had sneaked up behind Patty and tried to strangle her. Then he'd pushed her into the pool, just as we'd surmised.

Austin had been close enough to me when Tracey opened the door to him the day of my shower that he'd gotten a good look at my face, enough so that he recognized me after he delivered flowers to Megan at Lisa's house. I'd often wondered why he'd brought flowers to Lisa's. He finally admitted that he felt guilty because he'd learned that he'd killed the wrong woman. Maybe he had some sense of humanity, after all, although it was difficult to reconcile it with his murder of Patty and his holding me and Cole at knife point.

After initially denying that she'd hired Austin to kill me and that she tried to kill Austin, once he'd been named a suspect in Patty's murder, Smith clammed up, refusing to say another word.

Months later, we learned that Austin was scheduled to be the star witness in Smith's trial.

Chapter 25

When Saturday dawned, I resolved to put the events of Thursday morning out of my mind. It was our wedding day, Wes's and mine, and I wanted it to be as special as our love for each other.

Just because this was a special day for me didn't mean that Bear would be deprived of his morning walk. I tried to be as quiet as I could as I tiptoed down the hallway to retrieve Bear's collar and leash from their usual spot in the laundry room, but my mom had heard us get up, and she stepped out of the guest bathroom, already dressed to go with us.

"Your father's sound asleep," she whispered. "He may have overdone it a bit yesterday with the yard work, so I thought we'd let him sleep for a while."

I could hear Dad snoring softly. My parents had insisted on sleeping on the sofa bed in the den, even though I'd urged them to sleep in the master bedroom instead.

We quietly slipped out the side door of the garage to be greeted by weather that promised to be absolutely gorgeous. After the thunderstorms we'd had the other night, I'd been afraid that we might be in for a repeat performance on the Big Day, but the air was pleasantly cool, the lightening sky cloudless, and the air much less humid than normal.

My mother smiled. "Oh, I surely do hope the weather stays this good all day."

"So do I," I said. "Of course, it'll get warmer, but

let's hope, not too warm."

"It's going to be perfect. I just know it," my mother, the eternal optimist, declared. "I'm so happy for you. I don't suppose Wes would ever consider moving to Seattle."

"Oh, Mom. You know he has lots of years invested in his job, and moving now would affect his retirement pay. Besides, he's a native Iowan, and he's never expressed a desire to live anywhere else."

"His parents are native Iowans, and they're living in Phoenix."

"I know, but they're retired. Wes isn't planning on retiring any time soon. He's only forty-five."

"I suppose you're right, dear. I guess we'll have to be satisfied with visits. Why, we may even see you more than we would if you lived in Seattle. My friend Deborah's daughter lives in Seattle, and they hardly ever see each other."

My mother seemed satisfied by this thought, as we continued our walk, chatting about what we had to do to get ready for the wedding.

Dad was up and had already stripped the sofa bed of its sheets and restored it to its sofa status. While I started the laundry, Mom made oatmeal for him and squeezed fresh orange juice. She'd brought a new special blend of coffee for me to try. The enticing aroma wafted into the air, and I could hardly wait to taste it.

Mom insisted that I eat a bowl of oatmeal, too. After doctoring it with butter, brown sugar, and cinnamon, just like Dad's, she insisted that we all sit at the table in the dining room and relax over breakfast for a few minutes before preparations for the wedding activities started.

"Dad, I really appreciate all your hard work in the

yard yesterday," I said. "The lawn looks fantastic, and the bushes have never looked so good, trimmed to perfection."

"It was my pleasure, honey. How many people did you say will be here?"

"Not too many. Let me count." I mentally went over the guest list. Wes and I had decided on a small, informal wedding, and we had stuck to the plan. "Twenty of us, not counting the minister. She has to leave right after the ceremony to go to another wedding. She told me she'd be officiating at three weddings today."

"I think June's still the most popular month for brides," Mom commented.

Bear had been lying next to the table, but when Dad pushed back his chair, Bear jumped up, put his chin on Dad's knee, and whined softly.

"I think he's trying to tell me something," Dad said, stroking Bear's fur.

"What is it, boy?"

"That's Bear-speak for 'I want to go outside to play,'" I interpreted.

"Well, let's do that right now. Come on, Bear." They went into the backyard where Dad began tossing Bear's hard rubber ball to my eager canine. When Mom and I looked out at them a few minutes later, Bear was wandering along the perimeter of the lawn sniffing the grass, and Dad was following him with a shovel.

"It looks as though the guests won't have to worry about where they step," I said, "with Dad on the case."

"Don't you worry, honey. Your dad will watch Bear like a hawk. There won't be any unpleasant surprises."

"He really does think of everything, doesn't he?"

We laughed and went to work. I ferried our dirty dishes to the kitchen, and Mom put them in the dishwasher before she began pulling out pots and pans that she, Aunt Ellen, and Tracey would use when they prepared the food. She shooed me out of the kitchen, telling me that the only thing I should concern myself with now was transforming myself into a bride.

The next few hours passed in a whirlwind of activities, but whenever I came out of the bedroom to check on their progress, my mother or Tracey shooed me back into the bedroom. Meanwhile, I struggled to arrange my hair in soft waves.

Before I knew it, Tracey came in and reminded me it was time to dress. Wes had called, and he and his family were on their way.

"Let me help you with that," Tracey said, when I told her my hair wasn't cooperating. She grabbed a curling iron and, with a few deft strokes, had it looking just right.

"Wow. That was fast! I've been trying to fix it that way all morning. Thanks, Tracey."

"No problem. We'd better get dressed."

"First, Bear," I said. I opened the patio door and called him to come in. Dad had brushed him, and his coat looked well groomed and sleek.

As soon as he came in, I put his blue bow tie around his neck and fastened it in place. Then I put on his blue tux. The vest-like garment covered his chest. I'd designed to it to look like the front of a blue tux with a pleated white shirt in the middle.

"That is so adorable," Tracey said when she saw it. "He only wore the bow tie to the shower. When did you make his little tux?"

"Yesterday, if you can believe it. After I gave my statement to the state criminal investigator down at the station, I was so full of nervous energy, I just had to do something. Dad was trimming the bushes with Bear tagging along, and Mom was at your house cooking, so I had time to make it before we all went to Denise's for dinner."

I caught my breath when I heard Amber begin to sing the medley of love songs that she'd put together, especially for our wedding. Her husband Robbie accompanied her on his keyboard. He'd be playing the wedding march for us, too.

Mom came in to let us know Wes and his family had arrived. She helped me into my gown and zipped up Tracey's dress. While I was arranging the silk flower in my hair, she disappeared for a few seconds, returning with a black, rectangular jewelry box in her hand, which I recognized as the box in which she kept my great-grandmother's pearls.

"I want you to have these pearls," she said, opening the box and handing it to me. "I can see that they don't go with your gown, but you can wear them for some other occasion."

"Oh, Mom! Thank you." We hugged, but gently, so that we wouldn't have to repair our make-up. My eyes brimmed with tears, and Mom swiped some tears of her own from her cheeks, so we might as well have given each other a bear hug. We hurried to fix our make-up so that the ceremony wouldn't be delayed.

Dad opened the door to the bedroom and announced, "It's about time to get this show on the road."

Uncle Bill tapped on the patio door, and Dad drew back the shades. Uncle Bill tucked my mother's hand into the crook of his arm and escorted her to her seat in the front row. All the white garden chairs had been decorated with white and blue tulle; the minister stood beneath a bower of flowers and greenery that the colonel had helped Liz arrange; the guests were all seated; Wes, looking handsome in his navy suit, stood beside his dad.

Tracey stepped outside and nodded to Robbie, who began playing the wedding march on his keyboard. Everybody stood up and turned around.

"Come on, Bear," Tracey urged, and Bear jumped up to walk at her side as Tracey grabbed her bouquet.

Neither Tracey nor Bear put a step amiss as they slowly walked toward the minister. For the first time in his life, Bear heeled flawlessly. A ripple of laughter went through the crowd as they saw Bear in his mock tuxedo. I could tell Wes was struggling to keep from laughing out loud.

"Ready?" Dad said, extending his arm. "You look gorgeous, honey. Wes is a lucky man."

"Thanks, Dad." I kissed him on the cheek. "And I'm a lucky woman."

ABOUT THE AUTHOR

An instructor at five colleges over the years, Paula Darnell most often taught the dreaded first-year English composition classes, but she's also been happy to teach some fun classes, such as fashion design, sewing, and jewelry making. Paula has a Bachelor's degree in English from the University of Iowa, Iowa City, and a Master's degree in English from the University of Nevada, Reno.

Like Laurel, the main character in Paula's DIY Diva Mystery series, Paula enjoys all kinds of arts and crafts. Some of her memorable projects include making a hat and a cape to wear to Royal Ascot, sewing wedding gowns for both her daughters, exhibiting her textile and mixed-media artwork in juried art shows, and having one of her jewelry projects accepted for inclusion in *Leather Jewelry,* published by Lark Books. She sells some of her jewelry and hair accessories in her Etsy shop: www.etsy.com/shop/PaulaDJewelry.

Paula's interest in DIY craft projects and fashion led to her writing hundreds of articles for print and online national publications. She is the author of *Death by Association* and *Death by Design*, both in her cozy series, the DIY Diva Mysteries. You can visit her author website at https://www.pauladarnellauthor.com/ to read about upcoming books and subscribe to her Cozy Mystery Newsletter.

Paula lives in Las Vegas, Nevada, with her husband Gary and their 110-pound dog Rocky, whose favorite pastime is lurking in the kitchen, hoping for a handout.

Recipes and DIY Diva Projects

Iowa Beef Tenderloin and Pineapple Skewers

Tracey served these Iowa beef tenderloin and pineapple skewers at Laurel's shower. She used wooden skewers, but metal ones work just as well. If you use wooden skewers, soak them in water for half an hour before threading them.

Ingredients

1 pound beef tenderloin, cut into 1-inch cubes
1 red onion, cut into 1-inch squares
1 red bell pepper, cut into 1-inch squares
1 pineapple, cut into 1-inch cubes
2 tablespoons extra-virgin olive oil
2 tablespoons balsamic vinegar
2 tablespoons soy sauce
½ teaspoon garlic powder
½ teaspoon salt
½ teaspoon pepper

Mix olive oil, balsamic vinegar, soy sauce, garlic powder, salt, and pepper in a mixing bowl. Thread beef, onion, pepper, and pineapple chunks onto skewers and repeat in the same order until each skewer is full. Use a pastry brush to brush them with the olive oil mixture. Grill outside, using aluminum foil or a grill pan, or broil in the oven, turning once. Baste with the olive oil mixture occasionally during grilling. Grilling time is 8 to 12 minutes, depending on how done you want the beef to be.
Makes four servings

Alberto's Tomato and Burrata Bruschetta

Cynthia, Amy, and Jennifer enjoyed bruschetta as an appetizer, when they lunched with Laurel at Alberto's.

Ingredients

1 French bread baguette
1 cup heirloom, cherry tomatoes
1 ball burrata cheese
extra-virgin olive oil
1 bunch fresh basil
kosher salt
balsamic vinegar

Toss tomatoes with olive oil and salt and roast for 20 minutes at 400 degrees or until soft. Heat ½ cup balsamic vinegar over medium heat and simmer until it reduces to one-half volume and thickens. Slice baguette into ½-inch slices, brush with olive oil, and broil until lightly brown. Center of bread should be firm but not hard. Spoon tomatoes onto bread. Pull a piece of burrata and place it on top of the tomatoes on each piece, and then drizzle with the balsamic reduction. Sprinkle with chopped basil leaves.
  Serves four to six.

Pumpkin Cake with Cream Cheese Frosting

This recipe comes to us from Kate Schoenherr, a cozy mystery reader and a subscriber to the author's Cozy Mystery Newsletter. Kate says that her family loves this cake. She used to take it to tailgate parties for her daughter's field hockey team at Duke University, and all the girls loved it.

Although it's easy to use canned pumpkin for this recipe, if pumpkins are in season, you can use cooked and mashed pumpkin flesh, instead.

Cake Ingredients

3 cups all-purpose flour
1 ½ cups sugar
1 ¾ cup vegetable oil
3 ½ teaspoons ground cinnamon
2 teaspoons baking soda
2 teaspoons double-acting baking powder
1 teaspoon salt
4 large eggs
2 cups pumpkin (one 16-ounce can)
1 cup raisins or walnuts (optional)

Preheat oven to 350 degrees. In a large bowl, measure all ingredients except raisins or walnuts. With mixer on low speed, beat ingredients until just mixed. Increase speed to high and beat five minutes, occasionally scraping the bowl with a rubber spatula. Stir in raisins or walnuts.

Pour batter into a ten-inch tube pan. Bake one hour or until a toothpick inserted in the center of the cake comes out clean. Cool cake in pan on wire rack for a few minutes before removing it from the pan. Cool cake completely on rack. Frost with cream cheese frosting. Store in refrigerator.

Frosting Ingredients

2 three-ounce packages softened cream cheese
1 teaspoon vanilla extract
dash salt (optional)
2 cups confectioners' sugar
2 to 3 teaspoons milk

In a small bowl, with mixer on medium speed, beat the cream cheese, vanilla extract, and salt until smooth. Gradually beat in the confectioners' sugar and the milk until the frosting is a thick consistency for spreading on the cake.

Bear's Tuna Rice Dog Treats

Tracey enjoys making all kinds of dog treats for Bear, Laurel's lovable Labrador retriever. Tuna rice treats are among Bear's favorites.

Ingredients
1/2 cup water
1 5-ounce can chunk light tuna, water packed
1/2 cup instant rice
1/4 cup unsweetened applesauce
1/8 teaspoon cinnamon

Put water in saucepan. Open tuna can, leaving lid in place. Put the liquid from the tuna can into the saucepan by pressing it out with the lid. Bring to a boil. Remove from heat, add instant rice, and cover the saucepan immediately. Leave the cover on and let the rice cool to room temperature. When cooled, add the applesauce, cinnamon, and tuna and mix well. Pick up a rounded spoonful of the mixture, squeeze it so that it sticks together, and roll in a ball. Store in refrigerator for up to two days. These treats may also be frozen. If they will be frozen for a long time, wrap each ball individually in plastic wrap so that they won't become dry. Thaw frozen treats completely before giving them to your dog!

Makes about fourteen 1-inch tuna rice dog treats.
Tip: Using vinyl gloves when rolling the tuna rice balls makes the process less messy.

Bear's Bow Tie

Bear proudly sported the blue bow tie that Laurel made for him to wear to her bridal shower and wedding.

To make a bow tie for your dog, you'll need fabric, a sewing machine, and sewing supplies. One-quarter yard of fabric should be enough for even a very large dog. Depending on how much body your fabric has, you may also need interfacing. If you're using a lightweight, drapey fabric, you can use iron-on interfacing to give it enough body so that the bow tie doesn't droop.

You'll need to take some measurements to ensure that the bow tie is the right size for your dog.

Neck measurement: Using a tape measure, measure around your dog's neck, holding the tape measure as tightly as the strap for the bow tie will be. Record this measurement and add two inches to it. To determine the width of the strap, measure the width of your dog's collar, double it, and add half an inch. Make a pattern piece out of tissue paper, using these measurements.

Bow measurement: To ensure that the bow will be proportional to your dog's size, cut a rectangle from a piece of paper and hold it up under your dog's chin. Cut it to the length and width that you'd like the bow tie to be. Next, double the length and width measurements and add one half inch to each to accommodate the seam allowance. Make a pattern piece with exactly these measurements for the bow.

Loop measurement: Make another rectangle with the

first measurement the width of the original bow measurement (before you doubled it) and the measurement for the second side three inches. (The length may be adjusted in step 7.) Make a pattern piece out of paper using these measurements.

Pin the fabric to the pattern pieces, and cut them out; fold each lengthwise with right sides together, and stitch lengthwise with a one-quarter-inch seam.

Turn each tube so that right sides are facing out. A tube turner might help for the long tube, or you can pull the fabric through by fastening a safety pin to one end and pulling it through.

Tuck in the ends of the long tube about one-quarter inch and sew a straight seam across them close to the edge.

Flatten each tube, placing the seam in the center lengthwise, and iron.

Fold the two ends of the bow so that they meet at the center back.

Pinch the bow in the center so that little pleats form, and hand stitch them in place. It may help to wrap thread around the center first.

Wrap the tie loop around the middle of the bow, adjust the tightness, overlap the ends, and hand stitch one end over the other. If the loop is too long, just cut off the excess before you overlap and sew one end over the other. There should be enough space between the loop and the bow to slip the necktie piece through.

Slip the long necktie piece between the bow and the loop. Using the coarse side of the hook-and-loop tape, attach it to one side at the end.

To determine placement of the other end, put the bow tie on your dog and mark the spot for placement of the other part of the hook-and-loop tape on the other end of the tie.

Attach the soft side of the hook-and-loop tape at the other end. Now you can just press the hook-and-loop tape ends together to take the bow tie on and off your dog.

Birdcage Veil

Laurel showed the students in her DIY Bridal Crafts class how to make birdcage veils. These cute, retro-style veils are most often worn for weddings, but they can be worn on other special occasions, too, since French veiling is available in a wide range of colors. The only tools needed are all-purpose craft glue, a measure, needle, thread, pins, and scissors.

There are many ways to secure a birdcage veil in the hair. For this method, we're going to use a headband wrapped with embroidery thread. There are hundreds of colors of embroidery thread, which makes it easy to match the color of the headband to your hair or to match it to the color of the veiling, whichever you prefer.

Materials
15 inches of 9-inch width French veiling
1 skein embroidery thread
1 metal headband

Cover the headband with embroidery thread (use all six strands) by attaching the ends of the thread to the inside end of the band. Tightly wrap it, making sure all the metal is covered. End at the center top and glue in place. Cut ends neatly.

Repeat the process from the other end of the headband to cover the entire headband.

Lay French veiling flat and make a point two inches below the center top. Mark with a pin.

Thread the needle with thread to match the color of the headband. Secure the end of the thread to the veiling about one half inch from the bottom on one side. Going straight up, run a gathering stitch about three inches and then curve it over to end in the center. Leave a thread tail to gather the veiling later.

Repeat step 5 on the other side of the veiling.

Pin the lower edges of the veiling to the headband three inches from the ends of the headband. Pin the center top of the veiling to the center top of the headband.

Gently gather and adjust gathers along the headband and pin the veiling in place to the headband. Make sure the veiling is securely pinned before removing the gathering threads.

Sew the veiling to the headband with a tiny running stitch, making sure it's secure all along the headband.
Carefully trim the excess veiling from the side of the headband, making sure not to cut the stitching.

Optional: add a decorative silk or feather flower to the side of the headband and stitch in place.

Printed in Great Britain
by Amazon

42558740R00131